A love in Milan

ITALIAN ROMANCE STORIES
VOLUME 2

MADDI MAGRÌ

A love in Milan
Copyright 2023 Maddi Magrì
All rights reserved.
Translated from Italian by R. Ricci
Original title: Un amore in punta di piedi
Copyright 2022 Maddi Magrì
All rights reserved.

CHAPTER 1.

It would have been impossible to take a bike ride along the river that day. Impossible to leave the house. Impossible to stay at home as the air conditioning, crippled by its own maladies, lay dormant. A lone fan valiantly attempted to rouse some semblance of a breeze, but its feeble efforts only stirred the stifling air, like a weary sigh in the face of adversity. It was a stifling day, a day to endure.

In the midst of this languor, Francesca found herself ensconced in her favored baroque armchair. With a graceful nonchalance, her right leg rested upon the armrest, its leisurely motion akin to the rhythmic ebb and flow of the tides. The left hand, with a delicate grace, cradled a lipstick of cocoa butter, its case a trifling diversion from the listlessness of the day.

The hours of summer had transformed into an ordeal, a relentless parade of scorching days that left no refuge from their fervor. An African anticyclone held all of Italy hostage, Ravenna included. But

Francesca's personal tempest was of a different nature, a cyclone of circumstance that had battered her world less than two years prior, and whose tempestuous effects still reverberated within her.

The storm was one of financial ruin, her father's misfortunes casting shadows over her existence. Initially, the shock had paralyzed her, and her measured response had been a veneer of composure to combat the myriad troubles that had descended upon her. Only now did the true extent of the devastation begin to surface, just as the summer's heat left one fatigued and depleted.

Much like the merciless sun that drained her of energy, her father's financial collapse had stripped her of security. She retained ownership of a modest apartment, a glimmer of stability, but to salvage what remained, she had parted with cherished heirlooms. The humiliation of selling family jewels to unfamiliar faces weighed heavily upon her. The luxuries of yesteryear – the maid, the Mercedes, the Caribbean escapes – had vanished into memory's vault.

Yet, the greatest toll exacted was the vanishing of friends, those she deemed kindred spirits. Their comforting words, once a balm, now seemed as insubstantial as a wisp of perfume in the breeze. And then, her phone stirred, a trill that provoked a start. Each ring was a potential creditor's summons, a new claim on her diminishing resources.

Her phone was right on the side table and she sat as she was, swiping her fingers to view the notification.

It was a message. A confirmation to be precise.

Francesca had received the invitation to the high school reunion from her friend Sara a couple of months earlier, through one of the various social networks, which she now used in much moderation, after all that had happened to her.

The last thing she wanted, or better yet, the last thing she *needed,* was to attend her class reunion but when Sara had initially written to her and a small group, saying that she intended to organize a party, no one had dared to come out and reply that it was better to let it go. After all, if twenty years had passed and if the relationships had broken off, it was because no one had wanted to cultivate them. The others had replied with brief comments without emphasis, in all probability not to expose themselves too much. As for her, she had left an emoji: thumbs up; she hadn't felt like refusing, simply because it wouldn't have been polite.

She hoped that, in the end, the initiative would shut down due to lack of real support. And yet, that stubborn of a Sara had made it: she had managed to gather everyone's support.

Of the original twenty-three classmates of the

class of '02 of the Francis Bacon scientific high school, only two had declined. One due to health problems, apparently serious, even if Sara had asked her to send a video, to be viewed during dinner, and the other, Luigi, because he was unreachable. The family had told Sara that he had become a Tibetan monk and that he no longer used modern means of communication.

"I could more or less tell Sara that I have become a Buddhist too! Charity and chastity, here I am!" she murmured bitterly, throwing her head back.

Charity, for financial trials had woven an intricate web around her, and chastity, a result of a nuptial knot that had unraveled in the cruelest manner.

She curled up in a ringlet and stood thinking.

Facing her schoolmates was yet another test which she would more than willingly have avoided, in order not to have to submit again to competitive logics that no longer belonged to her, but which, she knew, would reappear.

At the time, she was considered the spoiled young brat and, truth be told, the classification suited her perfectly. It was a given that she and a couple of others at the school were members of the upper class, and since there was nothing she could do to change her status, there was no sense in hiding the perks that came with it. Starting with the guys who circled around her. Only of a certain level, handsome and attractive. Furthermore, Francesca wanted to move in a refined way in any circumstance, which only widened the gap between her and her former classmates.

With two of them, however, she had formed a deeper friendship. Giuliana, a curly redhead whose father was a manager in her family's business and Sara, who posed as a wealthy, without really succeeding. Her grandparents owned the most renowned delicatessen in the area, but this did not allow her to reach Giuliana's levels, let alone hers.

In the end, Sara was able to find her dimension. Mistress of the delicatessen, mistress of her own life. And also mistress of planning the reunion with old school friends. Probably a regurgitation of youth due to the dangerous approach of the infamous mid life crisis.

The cell phone vibrated and Giuliana Sgrò's name appeared.

Francesca sat up better and looked at the name for a couple of rings before answering.

From a friend from high school, Giuliana had turned into her divorce lawyer, defending her during her separation from Aldo.

Once they obtained their diploma, they enrolled at the faculty of law and initially shared that path, which Francesca had undertaken more for the advantage of not having to study alone, rather than for a real passion for jurisprudence.

In fact, with only but a few exams to go from writing her final thesis, she had abandoned her studies, preferring to continue her life as a future bride. Organizing a wedding, hers, had not been a simple undertaking, even if the dress, signed by a famous stylist, had been given to her by the editor of the magazine, *Sposa Mia*. As a result, she had needed to have the bridesmaids dressed by the same designer and Giuliana didn't mind at all.

"Giuli," she replied in a low voice.

"Hi Franci, I was calling you for the divorce papers and also... did you see the invitation for the class reunion?"

"Actually no. I was going to read it, but you called."

"It's the thirty-first."

"Ah right. Where?"

"In the farmhouse owned by Sara. Do you know the one towards Casal Borsetti?"

"Mm... is it in decent conditions?"

"I think so, she's renovated it. And it's nice, it's near the river."

"Okay...now don't overdo it. Last time I saw it, it was falling apart."

"Don't be so antisocial."

"Nooo. Of course not. I absolutely can't wait for the class reunion. I have waited for it all these years."

"Ah, ah, ah… you've got to admit, when Sara wants something, she gets it."

"A pain in the butt is what she is…"

"Have you seen the recent pictures of the others? I swear, Tiziana is unrecognizable."

"Is that a compliment?" Francesca asked, not even knowing who Giuliana was talking about. No matter how hard she tried, she couldn't remember a classmate with that name.

"I'll leave it to you to judge..."

"What did you want to tell me?"

"To get ready for Monday, not tomorrow, next week's. I haven't received confirmation yet, but the meeting should take place. At my office, at nine o'clock."

"Okay, but let me remind you that *he* requested it, not me. By the way, how are you going to dress for the reunion?"

"I think pants. I have to tell you the truth: I'm not too thrilled either… I have to go now, I have another meeting. Bye!"

Francesca closed the call and dedicated herself to reading the invitation.

'Hello everybody! The legendary class of '02! Can't wait to see you all on August 31st, that is, next Saturday, at my house, I'll leave you the address below! Please, be on time at eight! The catering will

cost us forty euros each, champagne included!'

Francesca hadn't drank champagne in a long time and with the sensation of cedar wood notes in her mouth, which reminded her of a vintage Dom Perignon, she began scrolling through the profile photos of the classmates with whom she had shared her teenage years. Some reflected the merciless passage of time, others were less ruthless.

"Aw, come on!" she exclaimed in surprise, as if she were still on the phone with Giuliana, "Tiziana! Now I remember! Aged... married... children... a classic."

She lingered and commented in a murmur, trying to associate the names with the faces she saw, but some people's memory just didn't want to know how to bring back some reminiscences. "This Massimo... Massimo Losi... who *is* he? Stefano instead, of course I remember you."

Stefano had been her first boyfriend, her first kiss. A crush that lasted for a couple of months, before dedicating herself to studying tirelessly for the final exams. After that, they no longer looked for each other and not feeling the need, Francesca left for the summer in Tuscany, leaving her first important story behind. The profile picture was from a few years ago and Francesca wondered if he had changed since then.

"Uff..." she continued, thinking that it would be hard to look him in the face, "Oh God..." she whispered touching the picture of another companion. "Is that David?!"

With David, on the contrary, the relationship had been different, a mixture of intolerant attraction, for the lack of better words.

"I hope to avoid him... oh, but will you look at that... Alessia!"

She immediately took her fingers away from the picture of her classmate, to weigh again that of David, not of the teenage student, but of the man. The picture was recent and time had marked his face. Forged would be the better word. The expression though, that hadn't changed. Still with eyes like a rascal and even the hair had remained in place, but tidier and with some gray strands. Neat and smiling. In her high school days, many girls had fancied him, but not her. She had always felt uncomfortable around him.

David's attitude towards her was strange, ambiguous. She laughed softly remembering an episode that had happened during recess. Francesca followed a dance course outside school, but when Professor Teodosi organized, for the Italian essay at the end of the second year, the representation of some poems dedicated to Ravenna, she asked her to accompany the declamations with a dance .

A few days before the recital, during recess, Francesca was talking about her ballet to other classmates, including Giuliana, excitedly expressing her doubts about the success of her performance. David was sitting in his seat and Francesca bumped her arm against him. She turned to apologize to him, but he stood up, looked her straight in the eyes and, blushing like a pepper, mumbled barely audibly: "Dance regardless of what's around you, Franci", and then quickly left the room.

Her classmates had laughed and, at first, she had hated him, because she had felt embarrassed by his unsolicited exit. She had joined her friends in teasing him, however, deep down, that whispered advice, hadn't gone forgotten.

"Good times..." she murmured, getting up and closing the social network.

She decided she would reply to Sara later. She had other things to think about: she intended to prepare the little speech she would have given to her ex-husband, for that umpteenth phase of the divorce.

The separation had been consensual, even if it was Aldo who had asked for it.

They had met during university and she fell in love with him almost immediately. Aldo was a handsome man, pleasant, not too clingy. In hindsight, it would probably have been better to marry someone who didn't play football with his mates every other day.

And yet, she had never been jealous. But

when she did discover the affair and asked Aldo for an explanation, she would have expected a different behavior, somehow she would even have forgiven him, maybe not enough to get back together, but it would have been enough to not start a war.

And yet the truth had been worse than the infidelity.

Not only had Aldo cheated on her with an office colleague, a rampant manager, but he had blatantly blurted out that her father's financial situation, suddenly in distress, did not allow him to lead the life he had imagined the day he had married her.

"So, you married me for the money?" she had asked him incredulously and Aldo had shamelessly told her the truth.

"Well, you didn't think I would embark on a marriage just for your pretty face, did you?"

Such a blatant statement of contempt, she would never have expected from her husband. And yet, Aldo hadn't had any scruples.

The sale of the apartment where they lived and the division of their assets, for Francesca, had taken place in a detached way, but Aldo had not given up on the issue relating to the maintenance allowance and therefore she had balked.

In fact, if at the beginning it was she who supported him financially and, later, thanks to her acquaintances, who found him the job as a manager, during this new phase, Francesca pretended that the her ex-husband was to repay her by ensuring she had enough to survive.

Do ut des, as the Romans used to say, not exactly the formula for eternal love, but, she considered bitterly as she got into the shower, this was the contract she had stipulated with Aldo: an impersonal return of favours.

The iced water of the shower gave her immediate refreshment. She passed her hand over her belly and over the scar, stroking it for a long time and together with the cold drops, totally apathetic tears fell down on the tub. Certainly, it wouldn't have been someone like Aldo who ruined her life. She was a survivor and as such she would react. Once again. She stared at that cascade of anguish leaving her body and rinsed as if nothing had happened.

Finally, she threw herself on the bed. She picked up her cell phone and replied to Sara's Whatsapp message, simply writing that she would be there and closed her eyes, trying to prolong the feeling of tranquility that that refreshing downpour had given her. The phone vibrated and she saw that Giuliana had answered after her, confirming her presence.

She was trying to go back to sleep, but repeated knocks on the door made her jump. It was about Aldo. She stood at the door, because she certainly didn't want to let him in and listened to his weak and insipid apology in silence, determined not to reply. The touch to the shoulder made her whirl around and she became aware too late of the woman attacking her. Her jaws engulfed her just like darkness engulfs light.

She woke up, panting, looking around to make sure she was at home, in her bed. Nightmares had become a habit and sleep a luxury which became harder and harder to afford.

The phone vibrated again. The notices of joining the class reunion had become insistent. She hit the off button, in order to go back trying to sleep again but not before seeing the Whatsapp profile picture of David, who had sent his confirmation message.

She curled up on her side and let out a long sigh.

CHAPTER 2.

"I fought hard to get those concessions when Fausto was still alive, you can rest assure I do not intend to give them up now, Giorgio!"

David stared hard at his employee and didn't drop his gaze.

"Fine, but know that we will have to fill out a lot of forms, probably submit new requests to the municipality…"

"Yes, Giorgio. We will have to work hard. As always. But the decision is taken."

Giorgio left the office and David stared at the door, his gaze absent and his memory going back to the day when he had met Fausto in the department head's office, for a few minutes, before the latter dismissed him hastily, pointing his pay and the time he was due to report the following evening.

For David, that night job as a guard had represented a significant increase in his income, but with a hard price to pay. The night trips between Milan and Cesano Boscone proved to be heavy and he had to do his best to fight his constant tiredness. He would leave his day job in Milan, where he worked as a computer technician and, on a motorbike, go to the factory in Cesano Boscone for his second job. He ate a sandwich and started the night shift. In the morning, he made the journey in the opposite direction, went home, washed, and after a quick breakfast, started again.

Continuing in that manner would have been impossible, and therefore he changed his destiny when he asked to meet Fausto again, the owner of the *Ditali e Filati* company, and he got himself a permanent job, preferring however to continue working on the night shift. During the day, however, he devoted himself body and soul to studying finance and business administration so as to learn the tricks of the trade in order to one day manage a business, his dream ever since he was a kid. The character of an entrepreneur was in his blood and it was innate, because although his father had a small shop of his own, it was certainly not he who passed it on to him. His old man was not the type to take risks just to earn a little extra, too busy making ends meet for a poor family, but one that probably oppressed him and David soon gave up any ambition to run the shop and turn it into an empire .

Fausto gave him the opportunity to test himself and give free rein to his dreams, because, in short, he granted him carte blanche on many issues concerning the company. The first decision that David made was to move the registered office of Ditali e Filati to Milan, in the Tortona area. It was not easy to convince Fausto to do it, but he succeeded by explaining to him that only by being closer to the fashion district, a melting pot of ideas and a source of inspiration, could one think of increasing the turnover.

Obviously, Fausto was used to moving exclusively within Cesano Boscone and David understood this. He had transformed his wife's small haberdashery into a real textile company, first working in the back and then expanding into a nearby shed and therefore he saw every change only as a big waste of time.

David on the contrary, after taking over the reins of production, had immediately understood that acting as wholesalers to other entrepreneurs in the area or, worse, selling those fabrics at retail, would have led the company to sure bankruptcy within a few years.

With dedication and strength of persuasion, he had forced Fausto to make that and other important changes and the latter had supported him, because he considered him as the son he had never had. David had exploited that weakness to his advantage, but still only and exclusively to improve the company. Loyalty was a principle on which he did not compromise and he loved Fausto as if he were his father. Perhaps even more than a father, Fausto had been to him a guardian of dreams and a mentor of destiny.

The building he had chosen, in Via Savona, had been built by an architect he had met during one of his trips in search of potential clients and his office almost entirely occupied the top floor of that high-tech structure.

He often savored that feeling of power that sitting in his armchair, behind the large glass table, gave him: he could not help but proudly think that the skinny little kid from the provinces had come a long way.

In those moments he also doubted that he could probably have done the same thing for his father's business, but after the usual careful analysis, each time, he surrendered to the evidence that their relationship had been difficult and that they had always been too distant to allow him to do what he had done for Fausto.

The only lesson he had learned from his old man was that customers had to be gained, aggressively, one after the other, and that was the main reason why he had insisted on moving Fausto's company to Milan.

Having moved the headquarters and enlarged the operations, the company Ditali e Filati had then specialized in ultra high fashion fabrics and for some years now had been a leader in the sector, collaborating only with the most exclusive brands.

Only one question remained outstanding. The name of the company had to be changed, made more captivating, but on that point, Fausto had been adamant and after his death, David hadn't felt like betraying his memory.

He rubbed his eyes and stared at the computer. Every day, he devoted ten minutes of his time to thinking of a new name and, each time, he closed the PC without having found a solution. Even that day.

He looked at the time. Half past eight. At home there was no one who would be waiting for him and he decided to take advantage and go downstairs to the company gym. One of the few luxuries he had allowed himself, but on the other hand, he considered it justified since he spent almost all his time within those walls. And the employees were happy too.

The gym was empty. He opened the door, stopped in front of the switchboard and turned on the lights.

He already had the playlist in mind to put on, but when he connected bluetooth to the amplifier, he changed his mind. Instinct was his best gift and he had always had the courage to support his choices, even if it was trivial, like songs to listen to during a workout. The sound system lit up, flashing to the music.

He turned up the volume, kicked off his shoes, tossed his duffel bag to the side of the ring and started bouncing left and right, hitting the air.

Although it was Sunday, he'd been working tirelessly since early in the morning that day, and his taut body barely responded to commands, jerking in defiance of what he wanted it to do. In spite of other days perhaps his muscles knew it wasn't a workday and that he should rest. Physical insubordination was nothing more than a kind of advice not to go overboard. However, he was not the type of man who gave in easily and therefore he supported his body, slowing down, but continued the training inexorably.

Even though he had turned on the air conditioning to the max, he could not calm the heat accentuated by his movements and, after a while, he had to stop to catch his breath. He leaned against the ring platform and opened the cap of the bottle with his boxing gloves on; by now, after years of practicing that sport, he was used to using bandaged hands.

The cell phone continued to vibrate and to bring up the confirmations of the class reunion that Sara had organized for the twentieth anniversary. He bent over to read as they scrolled across the display. Some were indulging in more friendly conversations, to pick up that thread that had been lost in the depths of adolescent insecurities.

David had accepted that invitation for two good reasons, one of which was that he would take advantage of the trip to visit an industrial site he intended to buy. It was a large shed on the banks of the Reno river, outside Ravenna. In those years he had expanded the business trying to limit fixed costs and a good solution had been to relocate production. The following months would be decisive and he couldn't afford to take steps longer than his leg, but neither could he stay still.

Like boxing, life, business and feelings had to be managed with mastery, a skilful dance back and forth, always on your toes, to deliver blows and dodge others. He had learned from the beginning that moving harmoniously would lead him to more effective lunges. Good grip on the ground was essential and for this reason he always trained barefoot, to feel the ground, so as not to be caught unprepared. To remind himself that, outside the ring, he always had to be on his guard and rely only on one being. Himself. And no one else in the world. He had quickly learned to manage loneliness. He believed certain emotions were superfluous, favoring hard commitment, which had always paid off and it was only thanks to his efforts that he had achieved success. In this, the discipline of combat had helped him, blazing a solitary path that he would never give up.

He resumed hitting the most relentless bag, knowing that he had a lot to unload and spent another good half hour pretending to strike fate, before returning to rest his elbows on the platform.

As he took off his gloves, his cell phone lit up and the picture of *her* appeared.

She was the second reason.

Or maybe she was the only reason. He smiled, took the towel, the bag, turned off the lights and went home.

The empty streets had never looked so good, and his body now docilely followed him as she shifted gears and swung hard at every corner. Every nerve knew that the day had taken on a new light and that he had been repaid in sacrifices just for having received that message.

He parked the car humming, munched on an energy bar and slipped into the shower, letting the cold water heal him. Once seated on the sofa, although it was midnight, he answered the message resolutely: 'See you on Saturday.'

CHAPTER3.

The recollection of the first day of school was etched into her memory, like a colored slip of sticky candy. Her schoolmates were complete strangers and she entered the classroom with the discomfort of someone who knows she has to start over to be accepted. Her proud intercession, however, immediately collided with the mischievous and intriguing gaze of a skinny boy, a little less tall than her, who embarrassed her so much that for the whole day she didn't dare to speak to anyone.

The reunion was for her a return to those annoying sensations and she looked at herself for a long time in front of the mirror before making up her mind.

She brushed her curls vigorously and pushed back that sense of bewilderment similar to that distant first day of high school.

Loneliness had haunted her for too long in the last couple of months and sooner or later she would have to throw herself back into the fray of life, so seeing familiar faces would have been a good starting point.

Sara's farmhouse was an old building, partially renovated, located along the Reno river, but further inland, towards the town of Mandriole. The clearing beyond the gate was very large and allowed her to park the car without great manoeuvres, far from other cars. Judging by the number, she must have been among the last to arrive.

She turned off the engine, just before another car pulled up alongside her. She tried to avoid looking to her left, but having to get out, she had no choice but to stare at who, driving a Seat Ibiza, had arrived with her. Fortunately, apart from not recognizing him, the man inside seemed interested only in adjusting himself in the mirror, so she too lingered to prepare herself spiritually, but jumped at the roaring sound of horsepower that came from behind her Lancia Ypsilon.

The fiery red Ferrari braked on the gravel just to her right and the man driving, took off his sunglasses and turned to look at her, smiling captivatingly.

"David..." Francesca murmured and reciprocated with a hint of a greeting. Both came out of their cars almost in unison and found themselves facing each other. They had shared school desks, but not the same friends and Francesca felt again that subtle distance that had divided them as teenagers. A gap linked to the families of origin and which they had mutually maintained, failing to free themselves from certain clichés imposed by life in the province. She was too high-sounding to make friends with the skinny kid who rode his bike all day long and who was the son of the shoemaker and therefore, although David had a magnetic gaze, she had always tried to avoid him.

It was David who distracted her from that series of considerations, breaking the ice.

"Francesca Novelli!" her pronounced her name emphatically, "How nice to see you!"

"Yes... nice to see you too and... well you made quite an entrance!"

"Ah, ah, ah…" David laughed, scratching his head and walked over to her. They shook hands and shared a light kiss on the cheek. Francesca blushed and was relieved to hear someone yelling from the porch: "You guys! You're finally here! God, it's been so long! Let me come and hug you!"

Sara hurried over to David, who answered with obvious embarrassment. "Sara... hi..."

"Francesca!" Sara said again, embracing her too, "It's been a while since we've seen each other! And… look who's there?!" He pointed to the other man who had arrived with them, but neither Francesca nor David seemed to share her memory.

"Massimo Lodi! Welcome!" she exclaimed

cheerfully.

"Ah, yes, Massimo, hello..." David seemed hesitant and, joining Francesca, opened the door of the farmhouse, saying: "Please, after you..."

"Wait," Sara stopped them, "You have to wear this around your neck! You two are on the same team. The fire one!"

"Wow, Sara", David said with a chuckle, "I am pleased to note that you haven't changed... you always organize everything... isn't it true, Massimo?"

"Ah, I... yes... well..." the man stammered very uncertainly.

"Massimo, you instead...", Sara handed him a badge holder with a stylized drawing of a sea wave inside, "... you belong to the water team..."

"Uh", David asked, looking mischievously at Francesca, "And what are we playing at?"

"You'll see, you'll see..." Sara replied, making an embarrassed laughter and entering the farmhouse, followed by the three.

The room was very large and, opposite the entrance door, a big fireplace occupied a large part of the wall. Despite the outside temperature, the fire was lit and a very long grill had been placed in anticipation of the meat. A caterer was taking care of keeping the flame alive.

"Oh, Filippo!" David separated from Francesca, who also moved away from Massimo, wandering away from the warmth of the fireplace and looking for a friendly face, as she had promised herself to do, but apart from Sara and David, the others suddenly seemed to her to be strangers, of whom she didn't know. Or care.

A peremptory voice made her turn around: "Aw, come on! Francesca, is that you?! You haven't changed at all!"

"Hello..." she answered shyly to the woman who had approached her with open arms and resignedly submitted to the squeeze.

"You don't remember who I am anymore, do you?"

"Ah, no, really, no... I'm sorry."

"I'm Lucia. Lucia Pitto. How are you?"

"Fine thanks. Now I remember. Chemistry experiment, Year Eleven, right? You were a phenomenon with the periodic table."

"Well yes. I made my life out of that passion. I am a pharmaceutical chemist."

"Wow, congratulations. I'm so happy for you."

"And you? What are you up to?"

The crackling of the fire in the grate made her jump, but it was the question that had stirred her up. Until that moment, she hadn't thought that anyone would ask her about *her*, about her present. Strangely, she convinced herself that they would only talk about the past, about anecdotes, about professors.

"I just got a job as a teacher. Substitute teacher, to be exact."

"I forgot that your aspiration was teaching."

"I had forgotten too apparently," she chuckled, "but in the end…"

"And where?"

"At our high school. Professor Giusti, who speaks Latin, needed someone she could trust and so..."

"Giusti?! She's still there? She hasn't retired yet?!"

"Just a couple of years left," Francesca answered, looking around for Giuliana. "Have you seen Sgrò by any chance?"

"The redhead?"

"Yes her."

"Well no. If she was here, she wouldn't have gone unnoticed."

"That's strange, I thought she was coming... I'll send her a message."

"Have you two stayed in touch?"

"Ah", she replied, reading Giuliana's answer, "Yes, with her yes... but it seems she can't come... sorry, Lucia, I'll call her."

"Go ahead and say hello from me."

She nodded and started to dial the number, but she saw Stefano and put the phone down, surprised. Time had passed on the man's skin, leaving him not only a white beard, but also a receding hairline that didn't help hide his age. The resemblance to the boy of the past was there, but Francesca didn't find any foothold that would allow her to match her memories with reality. The man recognized her and his eyes lit up as she waved at him. She came forward cautiously, because she felt that she couldn't help but show her amazement at seeing him again. Nor to hide her disappointment.

Her first love had lost in an instant the magic of those kisses stolen in the corridors of the school.

"Stefano"

"Francesca!"

Embarrassment took possession of them and they remained a few steps from each other undecided on the next words, looking for the best way to re-establish a relationship which, they both knew well, could not be revived, even if time had escaped the laws of the cosmos.

"I didn't think I'd be able to meet you... once again..." Stefano shyly approached and scratched his hand on his trousers and Francesca reacted with a couple of questions, instantly regretting it: "Yeah, me neither. How are you? Are you married?"

"Yes, ten years now. Two children, a third on the way. We are very happy."

Francesca noticed the emphasis with which Stefano had remarked on the last sentence, as if to underline his refusal to any hypothesis of adventure outside the marriage, as if she had proposed him who knows what and therefore she looked at him irritably, smiling in an affected way. "I'm glad to hear it. Very good. I think I saw… ah, yes!", she exclaimed, walking towards a group of men, "I'm going to say hi to David, over there."

She began to think that she had done wrong to attend the party, because all the memories were being ruined by the present and the brief conversations were causing her some discomfort.

Meanwhile, Sara spoke up: "Guys! Class of '02! I have assigned a symbol to each of you. Please look for those who are part of your team and regroup. Enough talk of the old days! We will resume later! And don't worry, I purposely tried to avoid redoing the groups from back then. Let's find out how we are today. We'll play a game before dinner to warm things up!"

"Uff", David turned to Francesca, as if he already knew she was there and unleashed a charming expression. The hoarse voice reached her sensually: "I have to tell you, Franci, that I'm afraid of Sara. I dare not imagine what she will make us do…"

"You're right", she replied with a smile, "she's always been crazy and in fact it's thanks to her that we're here today..."

"I find you very well, Franci…"

"Thank you…", she whispered softly, curling a ringlet. She would have liked to ask him how her life had gone on, but Lucia distracted her from the idea. "Here they are! Fire team, hip, hip, hooray!" yelled the woman followed by Filippo and Stefano.

David addressed a funny face to Francesca and whispered in her ear: "I remembered Lucia as shy and reserved and instead now, she's become quite the loud, loquacious type."

The tickle that those words had given her, combined with the good perfume that David was wearing, momentarily made her feel a sense of faintness, from which she recovered by brandishing the man's arm. They stared at each other and she babbled, "Oh, yeah… she's a chemist, apparently…"

"Mm…" David murmured thoughtfully: "…see what happens when you breathe too many solvents?"

Francesca let herself go to a hearty laugh and in David's gaze she found a completely unexpected complicity.

"Shh..." Lucia scolded them, "otherwise we don't understand the rules!"

They laughed again, but their classmate paid no attention to them, absorbed in listening to Sara, who continued to speak.

"... but, first of all, the representative of each team will have to come here and extract the theatrical scene that you will be called to improvise. Come on, come closer! Massimo, you start!"

The man took out a note and read aloud, shyly looking at the classmates around him: "Er, we will have to perform a funeral..."

"And no wonder, given his face," David murmured, chuckling.

"David!" Francesca took him back smiling, "You're being naughty...", she looked at him sideways and noticed his amber eyes shining, while he was muttering: "Who knows what they will make us do, Franci..."

Meanwhile, Tiziana waved the note for the air team: "We will enact a birth! Ah, well, I already know who will be the baby..." he pointed to a person at the back of the room: "Piero! You, without a doubt!"

A laugh accompanied her words and followed by the other four team members, she moved giving way to the representative of the fire team.

"Go Lucia, extract something interesting..." David urged her.

"Let's see..." she said, stirring in the jar and finally raised her arm, happy: "Wedding!" And immediately asked: "Sara we have to do it in a traditional way?"

"Whichever way you want it to be!"

"Oh, great! I already have an idea!" She raised her eyebrows and tugged at Francesca's arm. "You and I!"

"Mm… excuse me?"

"The two of us are getting married, Filippo and David will be the witnesses and Stefano will officiate the function. What do you think?"

The three men evidently nodded with little desire to stage any kind of union and therefore Francesca had no choice but to nod. "Okay…"

The skits followed one another amid embarrassments and laughter and when their turn came, Lucia settled down next to the fireplace, peremptorily indicating to her team members how to arrange themselves.

"Stefano, you in the middle and take these two, I took them from a couple of cans. For the wedding rings. Francesca, on the other hand…"

"Do I sit here?" she asked, but turned away feeling the ribbon in her hair pull. David had joined her and slowly letting go of the hair clip, muttered: "I think I'm going to be your best man", he smiled and whispered: "Remind me. How come you chose me? Am I your brother? Your friend?"

"I have no brothers…" she answered, drawing on reality.

"Ah, perfect, then I'm your best friend… even if, I'll tell you right away, it can't work between us like this; I don't believe in friendship between a man and a woman."

"I do, however. Otherwise I wouldn't have chosen you as a witness, would I?" Francesca looked at him with an amused expression.

"Mm... we'll see," he replied seriously.

Francesca was amazed at that affinity with David, who even seemed likeable to her and didn't shy away from an innocent game of complicit glances, while Lucia finished setting up the performance. "Filippo, you here. Stefano, get on a chair, so you'll be taller and they'll see you better!"

"Lucia..." Stefano asked grumbling, "I must say ladies and gentlemen, we are gathered here today to marry these... two... women? Is that all right?" he stammered, avoiding looking at his classmates and Francesca turned again to seek comfort in David, who grinned amused.

"Yes", said Lucia to the fake priest, "but be pompous, please!"

"So, then," Stefano hesitated, and David interjected.

"Do you know what you should do? Recite the formula of the past. You know the one with... if anyone knows there are impediments speak now or-"

"Oh, yes, yes, beautiful! Well done David!" Lucia clapped her hands and therefore, Stefano began the false ceremony: "Ladies and gentlemen!"

He addressed the audience, which raised a buzz and someone shouted at him: "Oh, Stefano! Ste!

Don't start preaching, like when we were young!"

"Shh…" he giggled and continued, "…we are gathered here today for Francesca and Lucia's wedding…"

Giggles rose and Piero commented: "Lucia… I expected it from you, but you Francesca… didn't you used to date the priest?"

Everyone laughed loudly.

"Ah, ah, ah…" Lucia turned and winked at Piero. It seemed that the two knew each other well and in fact the friend pressed: "Oh, Luci, then don't come and tell me that Simona is complaining, eh?"

"Don't you dare tell her…" they all laughed and Stefano stammered: "So, if there is anyone in this room who is aware of an impediment…" he raised his voice and concluded, "speak now or shut up forever !"

The members of the fire team turned to their classmates, including Francesca. The only one who didn't turn around was David, who, staring at her, emphatically stated: "Me! I know the truth! Francesca can't marry you, Lucia! Because in truth, she loves someone else! Me!"

And without waiting for anyone's reaction, David took Francesca's hand and dragged her towards the exit between the wings of the other companions, who stepped aside to let them pass. Someone started clapping, others laughed and a voice shouted: "How about the shoemaker eh? Nice twist! Well done!"

David and Francesca went outside and ran to the opposite side of the road, as if they were fleeing a calamity and stopped only near the river bank. Still hand in hand, panting, they looked at each other slyly and burst out laughing again.

"You saved me..." Francesca commented ironically. "For heaven's sake, Lucia is pretty, but..."

"Ha, ha, ha... well, if you say so! In my opinion, with this gimmick, we win the contest!"

"I didn't remember you so competitive, David..." she giggled, finally letting go.

"Actually, the intention was to escape this torture of games..."

"Yes, for me too, perhaps Sara exaggerated. This is a bit too much", she let go of his hand and they walked, one listless step after another, along the river. Every now and then they glanced at each other, their expressions contented.

"So, Novelli, what's going on in your life? How are you doing?" David finally asked, stopping and putting one foot on a low wall built to limit a piece of land. The moon illuminated his statuesque figure.

"Oh, well I guess, thanks Trilli. And you?" she added in a low and serious tone, "Listen, I wanted to tell you that... I was sorry to hear about your..."

David gave her an ambiguous smile.

"That's life. And then you too, your mom..."

"We lost them perhaps too soon."

"Mm... let's say that you and I didn't celebrate our twenty years brilliantly this year..."

Francesca looked at the moon and sighed: "No... a bad year. You were in Milan, right?"

"Oh yes. The fact that I was already away from home helped me, in a way. But a double blow... it was hard. First my father with that bloody accident and a few months later my mother. I threw myself headlong into work. That saved me."

"For me, it was different, I found myself alone with my father, who isn't exactly emotional, but what can you do? It is what it is..."

"And how is your dad? Does he still smoke cigars?"

Francesca smiled, struck by the fact that he remembered that detail of her father. "No not anymore. The doctor prevented him and so he became even more grumpy, if possible."

"Ah, ah, ah, but no, come on, he's a nice guy!"

"Oh, maybe because you had little to do with him, but I guarantee you he's a crazy pain in the ass. The older he gets, the worse it becomes!"

They laughed softly.

"I'm afraid," said David, "that I too will be that kind of father..."

"Poor daughter!" Francesca giggled again.

"You know, Franci", David became serious, "I miss Ravenna. Every now and then, I imagine myself staying here, maybe right next to the river, riding a horse, lying on the grass. I don't know... I've lost a lot of things that I could have had if I'd stayed."

"Well I, on the contrary, believe that I would have had a different life, if only I had had your courage, if like you I had gone away... I mean, of all of us, you are the one who has reached the highest success..."

"No, okay, don't overdo it..."

"Okay, I'll give you that. There are others as well... like our favorite chemist or... Piero", she pursed his mouth. "Did you see his arms?" His eyes widened and he laughed, scratching his beard, while Francesca continued: "he is so full of tattoos I don't think he has an inch of clean skin left. And that eagle on his arm in the long run will look like a plucked chicken..."

"Ah, ah, ah... I like his tattoos."

"Would you have one?!"

"Why not?" The amber of David's eyes gleamed, thanks to the reflection of the moon on the water.

"Because I think it hurts so bad!"

"Yes, but there are wounds that-"

"Hey! Guys! Come back inside!" Sara called them to order, interrupting that beginning of conversation. "The game isn't over yet!"

"Well Franci... I think there's no way to escape this agony..." he just brushed her waist, with the intention of crossing the road again and she let herself be guided towards the farmhouse, casting fleeting glances at him.

The games ended, their team won, acclaimed by the whole class, but during dinner they separated and Francesca remained at the side of Sara, Tiziana and Barbara with whom she spoke mainly of children and husbands, even if she avoided sharing her experiences , and just listened and nodded. Every now and then she looked for David, who, flanked by a couple of women, laughed heartily. She would have liked to stay at that table and participate in those apparently more carefree talks than those of her group, but she didn't have the courage to get up.

"What do you say, Francesca? Few of the men tonight can be saved, right?" Tiziana nudged her, "David is certainly one of them. Antonio too, over there…"

"Er, oh, I don't know… I…"

"Sara, didn't you date the shoemaker?" Barbara asked. "You let him slip... look how well he's grown there and from what I've heard he's also rich..."

"We were together for about three days. He left me because", she rolled her eyes, "he was in love with another…"

"I think that one falls in love easily!" Barbara commented and they laughed uproariously, with the exception of Francesca.

"Indeed," added Sara, "I'm glad it went the way it did. Do you know that he hasn't married? I, on the other hand, shortly after, found Tommaso. We have a nice house, our children... instead with that..." Sara didn't finish the sentence and the women turned to observe David.

Tiziana concluded on behalf of her friend: "I've heard his girlfriend is a foreigner, but they don't live together... well... how can it be done, I say..."

"Well, they're adults, they'll have their reasons, right?" Francesca replied annoyed by those gratuitous comments that her former companions were giving, judging a person they hadn't seen for some time. Her reflection extended to her life choices. She, too, she thought, would have been better off not marrying. Probably, she shared the same solitary approach to life as David.

"Yes, yes, he can do as he pleases..." Sara added. Francesca thought she perceived a hint of annoyance in her words, perhaps a regret, but the organizer of the class meeting changed register and stood up and ordered them and the others: "Everyone, can I have your attention! If we put ourselves there, the photographer will take the classic class photo! Ah, we have to repeat the one we did in the year of graduation which I sent you the other day, so settle down as you did then!"

The melancholy with which Francesca walked towards the wall was somehow quelled by David, who joined her and positioned himself behind her, squeezing her shoulder, while he chatted with his friend: "Filippo, you have to stay on my right. No, my right…"

"Ah, yes, you are right," Filippo said, looking at the old picture on his cell phone.

Francesca felt David's strong hand pressing gently and when the grip became slightly firm, she turned around. He slyly specified: "I was already taller than you, Novelli, of course, even today, I have to stay behind..."

"Easy, Trilli", she addressed him, "if you haven't noticed, I'm not short, just differently tall..."

"Ah, ah, ah… you're always the wittiest, Franci."

After the photos, the two mingled again among their former classmates, waiting for the photographer to distribute the various shots via social media, and they did not speak to each other again for the rest of the evening.

When Francesca decided to leave, she watched David from a distance. He was involved in an argument with three or four other friends. He looked serious, with assertive gestures. Very sure of himself.

Very manly, she thought. She would have liked to say goodbye to him, but she was too scared of slight embarrassments and misunderstandings and therefore she only said goodbye to Sara and her close friends.

"It's late, I'm leaving, thanks Sara, you really organized a nice evening..."

"Thank you, Francesca, for coming", replied Sara, who had stood up from the table to embrace her, "Tomorrow I will share on the group the other photos of the evening."

"Okay, bye!" she said and left. The cool air enveloped her and she shivered. She quickly slipped into the car and leaned her head back on the headrest as she thought about the strange evening and David. She had had fun with him, albeit sporadically and this gave her an injection of confidence for her sentimental future. "I just have to work hard to find a man who-"

Someone knocked on the window and she jumped.

"David..." she whispered, rolling down the window.

"Francesca, sorry, were you on the phone?"

"Oh, no. I..."

David didn't wait for an answer and accompanied his words with a sweet smile: "You too are tired of this party, aren't you? I saw you leave and... I wanted to say goodbye properly. After all, who knows how long it will be before we meet again. I would have liked to talk more with you... maybe next time..."

"Yes, me too… and… it was very nice to see you again. Truly. So… good night, David."

They stood looking at each other until David banged on the roof and babbled, "Good night, Franci, take care."

She followed him from the various mirrors and saw him get into the car. She waited for him to drive away before shifting into reverse.

CHAPTER 4.

From the conversations with his former schoolmates at the reunion the night before, David had gleaned some information about their current lives, but from the only person he really wanted to know something more, he had not been able to get anything.

And a slight sense of bitterness had remained. Truth be told many years had passed and he felt like a fool for having hoped for a different conclusion. He consoled himself by strolling through the streets of Ravenna, and of what he considered to all intents and purposes his one and only true home.

The Piazza del Popolo embraced him with a blend of familiarity and change, as if time itself had woven a tapestry of memories and evolution. Having grown up within its cobblestone confines, the square held a mirror to the young soul that had once roamed its ancient arches, and now, returning as a visitor, those reflections danced with poignant clarity.

Passing through the arches that guarded the piazza, David was enfolded in an embrace of wistful remembrance. The sights that had once been daily companions now stood as silent witnesses to the passage of time. The Fontana dei Leoni whispered secrets from its flowing waters, recalling laughter and whispered conversations that had long since faded into the tapestry of the past. The buildings that framed the square bore the scars of countless seasons, standing as steadfast sentinels to the evolving chapters of life.

The grandeur of the Duomo still commanded reverence, its mosaic-adorned façade a testament to centuries of devotion and craftsmanship. As David looked up, the intricate tiles seemed to spark memories of youthful wonder, a time when the stories they depicted were as vivid and alive as the present moment. It was a link to the innocence of childhood, a connection that bridged the chasm between then and now.

Surveying the scene, a wave of nostalgia washed over David. The memories of clandestine rendezvous with friends near the Fontana dei Leoni, the nights spent lost in conversation beneath the shadow of the Duomo, and the exuberant festivities that once filled the square with joy all surged to the forefront of his mind. He couldn't help but reflect on the innocence of youth, a time when the square was a canvas upon which friendships, crushes, and dreams were painted with the brushstrokes of shared experiences.

Leaving Ravenna had been a rite of passage, a step toward growth and self-discovery. The vibrant energy of Milan had become a part of his identity, yet Piazza del Popolo remained a touchstone, a symbol of the roots from which he had sprung. Standing there, basking in the mosaic of memories and emotions, David understood that Ravenna would forever hold a piece of his heart, a cherished chapter in the story of his life.

By bike, he had cycled the Piazza many times as a kid, back and forth, in summer and in winter, early in the morning, before starting school and sometimes in the afternoon, if his father asked him, to make the last deliveries.

The shop, which his father had inherited from his grandfather, was, according to the family's plans, destined for him. But his plans were different from those of the family.

He stopped in front of a shop window and stared blankly inside. He knew he had displeased his father, but at nineteen, after graduating from high school, he didn't and couldn't remain locked up in that little corner of the world. He neeed to live where things were happening. Where energy flooded the streets.

A backpack, some money in the pocket and Milan as the only possible destination.

He was reflecting on his choice, impulsive, but which had paid off, when he was distracted by a scent. *Her* scent. He observed the Piazza from the reflection of the window display and saw her coming.

David smiled.

No matter how many years passed, he would always recognize her scent anywhere in the world. In fact, he still felt it on him from the previous evening. Since the first day of high school he had tried to be close to her. He simply could not help himself, attracted as he was like a bee to a precious flower. He chuckled as he remembered how every year, he didn't pick a seat until he was sure where she would sit and only then would he take the desk behind hers. In year eleven or twelve, he had found himself begging someone else to switch, so that he was behind her. Years spent observing her curls so soft, her neck so delicate, her cheeks and smile, so intriguing. He had pledged that she would consider him, but he knew that in her eyes he would always remain the shoemaker's son. And she, on the other hand, was Novelli's daughter. A princess, who would never give credit to a cheap toad like him.

In fact, Francesca had a natural predisposition to be elegant and impeccable and even now, where she seemed agitated and talking on her cell phone, her movements had a class that he thought was admirable.

She was coming under the arcades, where she

had stopped, and so David began to hear parts of the conversation she was engaged in.

"... What?... and since when, sorry? No, listen, I repeat, it was *he* who wanted to see me and who had set for tomorrow. Certainly not me... in fact... yes... yes... no."

Francesca stopped before the arch and David saw her take out a tissue and start talking again, sobbing: "What?! You're joking, right?! Oh God, Giuli, he can't do this to me! He can't treat me like this! After all I've done for him! And you... you... aren't agreeing, by any chance?! What do you mean there is nothing we can do?" she mumbled, asking the question expressionless and throwing her head back. Her curls had descended on her back, but a ringlet insisted in front of her and it was when she answered again, bringing her torso forward, that even that last tuft of hair moved aside, completely revealing her face.

Amidst a life adorned with fleeting connections, David had encountered many women whose allure was undeniable, their youth and beauty casting an ephemeral spell. Yet, amidst this tapestry of experiences, Francesca's countenance stood out like a precious gem in a sea of stones. Her face, to him, was akin to a masterpiece painted by Botticelli himself – a work of art that transcended mere aesthetics and resonated with a deeper, more profound truth.

Her features, delicate and angelic, bore a symphony of details that unveiled a beauty untouched by artifice or pretense. It was as if nature had taken her essence and painted it upon a canvas of flesh and bone. Each curve, each line was a brushstroke, carefully chosen to create a composition that spoke of authenticity and grace. Her beauty was not just skin-deep; it was a reflection of her soul, an embodiment of the purity that resided within.

And then there was her gaze, a window to a realm of emotions and thoughts that beckoned David to explore its depths. Lively and spirited, it held a spark that danced with life's fire, an indomitable spirit that mirrored the vitality of her very being. The intensity of her gaze had a magnetic pull, drawing him in like a sailor enticed by the siren's song. Even now, as he found himself separated from her by distance, he could still feel the electric charge of her presence, as if her gaze had a timeless reach that transcended the confines of space.

"I don't understand anything, Giuliana! I do not want you to give in to his requests! You have to do something! Please, you have to do something! He can't do as he pleases he's a... aaargh!"

The years spent playing baseball in Ravenna had endowed David with a natural predisposition for reception and in fact he had been one of the best catchers on his team and therefore, although decades had passed, when Francesca impetuously threw her cell phone towards the window, he reacted promptly: he turned around and with an athletic leap managed to catch the object in the sky, before it shattered on the ground.

David first looked at the hand, then Francesca who, fists at her sides, had bowed her head and was staring at him in amazement, weeping silently. Finally he looked back at his hand; the throw had been violent.

An excellent pitcher could have sent an object traveling more than a hundred and fifty kilometers per hour. Francesca, thanks to her rage, had probably touched thirty, forty kilometers per hour.

David snorted, thinking that with this experience, he fully understood the importance of wearing a baseball glove. Now his fingers, due to the good throwing of Francesca, were suffering from that lack of protection.

"David!" Francesca approached cautiously and still shaken by the conversation she had just had. She sighed. In the meantime, a distant voice was calling her name from the cellphone: "Francesca? Are you there? Francesca please... let's talk about it. Franci?"

David bent his mouth forcing himself to smile and handed the mobile phone back to Francesca, who answered the imploring voice: "Giuliana... no," she kept swallowing, to try and stifle her tears, in vain, "I'll... call you... later ."

David observed her while rubbing his palm and commented: "You should have played baseball with me, you would would have made a damn good pitcher..."

Francesca didn't even try to answer cheerfully. Those words were like a dam whose barriers suddenly open, releasing the entire body of water. She began to cry profusely, trying in vain, to wipe the tears off her eyes.

"Oh, no, no, come on, wait. Franci. Wait," he patted her cheeks dry with his cotton handkerchief.

"Sorry, sorry..." she babbled, "Oh God, I'm ruining your handkerchief and..."

David put his still-aching hand on her shoulder. "Franci, it's me... you don't have to apologize. Come on, take the handkerchief..."

She nodded, accepting the offer and he continued: "Actually, you know what?" He tried to be cheerful, even though the pain was still present in his hand: "How about we have breakfast together? I was about to go to the bar..."

"Ah, no, no... don't..." Francesca blew her nose and added, "I don't want to ruin your morn-"

"You're not going to ruin anything. And after all," he chuckled, winking at her cell phone, "you owe me. Don't make me pray, it's on me and... uff, you don't want to leave me all alone to have my last breakfast in Ravenna, right?"

"Are you leaving? Already?" Francesca realized that the question was redundant, but David answered anyway.

"Yes, I should be in Milan in three hours, but I didn't feel like leaving without first taking a last stroll. You know, old memories, old friends..."

"You can save the old friend bit for someone else! I'm not that old yet!" Francesca laughed sincerely.

"You're right. My bad. Come, my dear *young* friend, let us go to the cafe."

"No, not here, God forbid", Francesca replied, "The espresso is absolutely undrinkable. Beyond the church, there is a bar with specialty coffees and where they have delicious croissants."

"Well then let's go, Novelli, what are we waiting for?"

Francesca made a slight forward movement, awkward, and David gave way to her, flanking her and remaining silent.

He intended to enjoy the walk through the streets of the center of Ravenna, imagining himself the protagonist of another life. A life lived in the provinces, with church bells in the background and a wife to share small festive joys. A wife like her, elegant, polished, refined, of a higher class than him.

And perhaps a bit of a socialite. Yes, he wished he'd married a woman like her. Or rather, he wished he had married her.

Francesca distracted him from his improbable thoughts.

"I didn't want to throw the phone..."

"You don't have to explain yourself to me. You must have had your good reasons. Besides, if he's an asshole, he's an asshole," he turned away smiling, holding the bar door open for her to enter.

"Well, he's..." Francesca didn't finish the sentence.

"Don't think about it," David told her and walked over to the counter. "Hello. We'll be sitting over there, could you bring us..." David looked at Francesca, who whispered the word espresso and therefore looked back at the barista, "a cappuccino, an espresso and a selection of croissants. And some mineral water too, thank you."

"Coming right up!"

"Come, Francesca", David moved the chair to make her sit at the corner table.

"I didn't remember you being so polite..."

"I'm not, of course. I'm just trying hard for you, Novelli."

"You're kind to force yourself", Francesca touched a ringlet, showing a certain shyness. David sat opposite and said nothing and while she was trying to fix her make-up, looking at herself in the small mirror, he continued to fantasize about the life he wished he had had with her. He was so engrossed in the story he was making up that, when the bartender served the croissants, he wanted to impress Francesca.

"Excuse me, can you bring me a pen as well?"

"Sure," he replied and meanwhile David said to Francesca who was looking at him curiously: "I'm quite sure I can guess the croissant you'll choose", and, having got the pen, he wrote something on a napkin, then folded it and seraphically muttered : "Take your croissant, then read aloud what I wrote."

"What if you're wrong?" Francesca asked, challenging him and waving her handkerchief.

David denied with a mischievous grin. He closed his eyes, took a sip of cappuccino and commented: "Trust me, I'm not wrong."

Francesca didn't lower her gaze and took the only croissant without any filling.

David's scream filled the bar: "I knew it!" He slapped the table and addressed the bartender he ordered: "Excuse me again, can you bring us a teaspoon? Indeed, no, better two. And a knife and a saucer. Thank you."

"What do you need them for?" asked Francesca, who still hadn't taken the croissant.

"Franci, you're so predictable," he replied,

"Either that, or I'm a genius."

"Mm… I'm not predictable."

"You are right, it's not you, it's me. I'm a genius."

"That's not what I meant," she said smiling.

"Really? Well then, why don't you read what I wrote?"

At that point, Francesca could do nothing but open the napkin and despite herself had to admit that yes, indeed, she was predictable.

"Loud, Novelli, please…"

The grimace that came out in return made David laugh heartily: "Ouch, I made Novelli angry. Remove the knives, otherwise if she throws those instead of the phone, people are going to get hurt!"

Francesca folded her mouth and let out a half smile.

"All right, Novelli, I'll tell you", he said as the waiter brought what he had asked for. "Oh, thank you!" and he continued his explanation, placing the small plate in front of Francesca.

"You would have preferred this croissant right here, with the cream inside", he cut it in half, "and also this one here filled with chocolate", he continued, while also dividing the chocolate croissant in two and arranging the two pieces on the plate, "however, since you are afraid of getting the cream and chocolate all over your pretty dress, you opt for the empty croissant. Hold the two teaspoons to prevent the cream or chocolate from falling on your dress, princess. Plus, you won't feel like you're eating too much, since I'll sacrifice myself and take half of them from you. But please, do me a favor, leave that dull empty croissant and opt for something richer..."

The saucer with the half croissants from which the creams poured out and the spoons arranged by David in favor of Francesca looked like a work of art.

"I'm only answering your insolence because you're making fun of me in a polite way..." she began and he scratched his beard, happy to have somehow conquered her.

"Let's hear it, Novelli..."

"So, Trilli, first of all, I don't like cream... I'd take the chocolate, but I won't eat it because I don't intend to gain weight. Age already is taking care of that", she said, tasting the stuffed croissant. "Lately, I've been quite depressed and if I were to listen to my food cravings, the scale would break."

"I'm sorry... what's wrong?"

A car passed by and Francesca turned, then sighed and stared at David. He reached down to her arm and took her wrist. The teaspoon he was holding wobbled.

The last thing he wanted was to make her angry. "I was stupid. Forgive me."

"It's not you. You ended up in this story

because, to be precise, I involved you, throwing the cell phone. You saved it from a thankless end. And if it had happened, it would have been yet another defeat for me."

It seemed to David that Francesca was hesitating in revealing the truth to him and he tried to push her to open up.

"Matters of the heart?"

"Yes and no," she allowed herself another spoonful of chocolate cream, without David taking his hand off her wrist. She let him.

"You know, I read somewhere that there are only three issues which deeply affect our lives: love, health and money." He emphasized the word money.

The tears returned and at that point Francesca freed herself from her loose grip, to retrieve the handkerchief from her purse.

She nodded and muttered, "It's been a hell of a year, David. I don't know if you've heard this, but suddenly my father found himself unable to sustain what he considered his personal empire. I..." she dried her tears and muffled a moan, "I've never taken the reins of the company and I don't know if it was a question of wrong choices, lack of vision, wrong advice given by unscrupulous people, but out of the blue what was clear before suddenly became dark. And Aldo, my ex-husband-"

"The asshole?" David asked with an innocent

look that made Francesca laugh.

"Ah, ah, ah, yes, he… he dumped me, because I discovered that, in reality, he had married me exclusively for the money. After so many years, he put the icing on the cake of all my troubles and it was bad. We sold the house and with that money I bought a small apartment, but I had to give up the life I was leading before. A little less than a month ago, I found a job. Nothing special."

She stopped and looked at him, exhaling strongly, before starting again: "Latin substitute teacher at our old high school, to scrape together something. I was supposed to start in a couple of weeks, with the new school year starting, but he… the asshole…" she laughed, "he found out and won't give me any more alimony and according to my lawyer", she didn't tell him her lawyer was Giuliana, "he's right and the Court will order the revocation."

She then turned silent and looked down. David did not say anything.

Finally she said, "Well… thanks for listening, David… it was just an outburst, I'm sorry if I-"

"Listen Franci", David interrupted her. "Why don't you come work for me?"

The question surprised even him; it came out instinctively.

"David…", Francesca began, but he interrupted her again. He was going to do something for her. Anything.

"I know what it means to live in the province and be on everyone's lips. Just because you know each other or, better, because you think you know each other, because, for example, your grandmother and my grandmother went to mass in the same church, then each believes they have the right to judge. In my opinion, you should get away from Ravenna for a while. I'm not saying forever, but long enough for things to calm down."

Francesca leaned back and examined David.

To David it seemed that her perfume had become even more intense and he looked her up and down, inebriated.

"David, you are really very kind, but what could I do for you?"

"We currently have an opening for the position of chief of staff… to the office of the Chairman." He had just made that position up. "The Chairman being me."

Francesca laughed throwing her head back and had a hard time calming down.

"Oh God," she wiped the tears from her eyes, this time from hilarity, "One thing I have to thank you for, there's no doubt, David. You have given a different twist to my day. Really, thank you," she said and touched his arm.

"I'm serious, Franci," he took her fingers and

squeezed, "I offer you this position because I think you might be able to help me. Do you know what I do?" He didn't wait for her to reply, "The early days in Milan were tough. I had two jobs. One, during the day, which exhausted me and gave me little satisfaction, and, after dinner, an apparently bland job, but which in the end determined my destiny."

Francesca leaned towards him, leaving her hand in his, and asked curiously: "And what was your job?"

"I was a night watchman in a small textile company. I slept very little."

"Ah, well, I couldn't have, if I don't sleep my seven-"

"No, in the sense that every evening, I studied the manuals of the machinery. In short, I learned all about the production chain and asked the owner to let me work as a laborer at night. At first, he, who was a very attentive man to his employees, was not very inclined to make someone work late, but later, also thanks to the pressure of the other workers, he gave in. We also began to weave at night."

"So you are an exploiter... I'll have to keep that in mind, if I want to accept..."

David chuckled: "Those men were happy to earn some extra money and besides, we organized production better and the company grew. I made a career and became CEO. When the owner died, his widow handed over the business to me. They had no children and I carried it on as if I had created it."

"Wow, I'm impressed!"

"Yes, I say that without false modesty. Currently, my company supplies the most well-known fashion brands and this is where you come in."

"David, you know I have no experience in the industry."

"Oh, yes you do. I deal with celebrity designers of the caliber of John Boyde, Antonio Lo Pace, Peter Hogen, Annalisa Damiani. Established and emerging stylists, but all successful. You know how to talk to people like this."

She raised an eyebrow, "David, talking to people isn't hard, and you're telling me you don't have anyone up for the... role?"

"You won't believe it," he made up an excuse on the spot, "but I've tried with young people, more experienced professionals, men, women, but the reaction is mostly one of awe. Conversely, those with experience in public relations turn out to be... too arrogant or too tied to patterns that they have been taught in school notebooks. I need someone I can trust and who really knows how to handle certain... situations. You learned it in the field, you are intelligent and insightful."

"David, you don't know me..."

"You mean I'm wrong about you? I don't think

so. In this job, you often have to know how to make decisions quickly, without my consent. In two weeks, Milan will host the fashion show and it will be like hell on earth, I won't deny it, but in my opinion, having you on board will only benefit me. The more I talk about it, Franci, the more it seems to me like a fantastic idea."

He picked up another napkin, scribbled something on it, and turned it towards her, pointing his fingers, gnarled and strong, to the sides to keep it taut as she read. Francesca didn't remain impassive, she looked up and opened her mouth, but it was he who commented.

"This is the salary, there will be a profit-related bonus which will be decided in due course. There are other benefits, such as welfare, that the human resources manager will be able to better describe to you. You will report directly to me and in turn have assistants. In short, we would be a team."

David finished talking and savored his breakfast together with the expression of Francesca who, still incredulous, ran her fingers, with pink-painted nails, over the napkin.

"David I... I don't know if I'm able to..."

"I know it may scare you, but I will be by your side, as long as it takes," and that, David thought, was the only thing that really mattered to him. Support her in a difficult moment.

Francesca seemed conflicted. "Milan… I don't have a place to stay there…"

"I have an apartment in the center. Small, which we use occasionally, to host clients. You'll stay there until you've settled in and calmly found something more suitable."

"I don't even have a degree..."

David laughed. "Franci… do you think that someone like me is interested in something you have studied or have not studied? You have character. You had it when you were, no offense, younger, and you proved it to me this morning. Who is the woman who throws an object away with that power? Just one who has no fear. And your opinion about my offer is only related to the image you have of me. If someone else you did not know had offered it to you, I'm sure you would have accepted immediately. Put this life behind you, not just your cell phone. Leave with me today. Time to pack your bags and you'll be in Milan tonight. Away from what makes you sick."

Francesca's sigh resembled a surrender. She kept turning the napkin over and over and shifted her gaze from the white of the paper to the hazelnut of David's eyes.

"You're not kidding, are you?"

"Why should I be?"

"I don't know. I'm asking you. Should I worry?"

David shook his head and took out his cell phone, but kept his eyes focused on Francesca, unknowingly sharpening her discomfort. He had to convince her and made a call.

"Micaela? Hi. Yes. Yes, everything is fine. I'm coming back today. Look, I just hired someone to be chief of staff. Yes... no... no, he doesn't know, yet. Well, I'll sort it out when I get back..." he murmured and saw Francesca, who was watching him with big bewildered eyes.

In that instant, David realized he had screwed up. How could he have said those things just to make her happy? Hire her, just to have her close. He had gone mad, but he couldn't help but follow this whim.

On the other end of the phone, Micaela's ringing voice brought him back to the floor: "Hello? David?"

He replied: "Yes, sorry... her name is Francesca Novelli. I'll pass it to you now. Can you please outline the contract she will need to sign? I agreed the amount with her... yes, I'll send you an email with all the details... oh and one last thing. Ms. Novelli will stay in the company apartment in Corso Magenta. I need the keys. Would it be possible for tonight? Otherwise I'll find another solution... ah... okay... thank you, um... you are a sweetheart. Perfect. I'll text you as soon as we're around. I'll pass you... Francesca, hold on. It's Micaela Stormi, our head of HR."

Francesca's fingers trembled and David's smartphone almost ended up in the glass of water.

"Sorry," she said, brushing his palm and stuttering, she replied, "Hello? Pleasure to meet you. Er… I think… yes. Yes."

Francesca's silence was filled by David's voice who asked for the check. While he was busy paying, chatting amiably with the bartender, Francesca listened carefully to Micaela, who provided her with details that she wasn't used to, because that would be her first real job.

"Then tonight I'll have the pleasure of meeting you personally, it seems," Micaela was saying, "I'll leave you the keys to the apartment. The company keeps a copy for obvious reasons, but you don't have to worry because they are locked in a safe and no one is authorized to use them, unless there is an emergency.

"Oh, yes, well, indeed, it's better that way. You never know."

"Indeed! Once the basements were flooded and we had to run to understand if ours too was among the submerged ones… ah, ah, ah."

"Mmf..." Francesca tried to laugh, but frowned.

"Goodbye Micaela", she handed the cell phone back to the owner and assumed a firm tone: "David?"

"Tell me, Franci."

"I can't accept. Thank you very much for thinking of me, but I'm out of time for things like this... your offer is generous and-"

The moment was crucial and David thought he should use it to his advantage. After all, being an intelligent woman, Francesca too had realized the madness, the absurdity of that drama and it would have been easy to indulge her, getting out of the impasse without feeling too bad.

Yet her perfume, her smile, bewitched him. Francesca was playing with a curl and David understood that it was he who needed her. He sighed and traced his line resolutely and aware that, afterwards, he would not have retraced his steps, nor would he have wanted it to go any other way.

"Oh no, Franci! You're not in a position to refuse and you know why?! Because I'm sure of one thing, I can see it in your eyes: you want to try, you can't wait to throw yourself headlong into a new adventure, because you're tough, you're someone who accepts challenges, who takes the bull by the horns, like me, so now let's get out of here, let's go to your house, I'll wait for you in the car and you calmly pack a couple of suitcases. Oh and, well, don't pack too much stuff as I don't have much space in the car", he chuckled and meanwhile, he had an idea to give both of them a way out, in case it was necessary: "Tell you what: tomorrow morning you start and stay for a week. If either of us still has any doubts by next Friday, I'll take you back here and it will be as if nothing had happened. But today, I'm not leaving without you, Franci."

CHAPTER 5.

It was not yet past twelve that they found themselves at Francesca's house, ready to leave Ravenna.

"So... I'll wait for you down here, Franci," said David while smiling.

Francesca rushed up the stairs, reflecting on the fact that in any case it was true that she had accepted precisely because of the frankness with which David had spoken to her. She was extremely convinced of the sincerity of his words, because, according to her, his lively gaze did not lie.

Generally, during her previous life, Giovanna would have been there to take care of closing the house and this was an aspect that had not occurred to her, sitting at the bar table, so when she entered the house, she organized herself to avoid making David wait too long.

Resolute, she grabbed a black bag and opened the fridge. She threw away whatever came into her hands and that gesture immediately made her feel good. She was closing with her past and embracing her future. She even began to whistle as she rinsed the dishes and turned off the electricity. After that, she devoted herself to preparing her things: her necessaire, which she placed inside the Louis Vuitton bag, large enough to fit four suits, one of which was a tailleur, five shirts and three pairs of high heeled pumps. Basically, the only elegant clothes she had left, stuffed into the only suitcase she had. The rest, she had sold on one of those branded vintage clothing sites. She added underwear, pajamas, two pairs of tights. Anything else she needed, she would buy in Milan.

She closed the front door and didn't stay even for a moment in front of the door to avoid having second thoughts and was shaken by a laugh of which she wasn't even ashamed when, on the stairs, she met the elderly lady Bergamaschini.

"Until we meet again!" she saluted her cheerfully and continued to descend quickly towards the door. She gave David a huge smile.

"Are you happy?" he asked, holding the hood open.

"Yes, David, very much!"

"Good! Let's go!"

The street was surprisingly light on traffic for a Sunday. "We are lucky, it is the first of September and people have already returned to the office last weekend, otherwise, it would have taken us at least two hours longer than expected. If you don't mind, I'll leave the music on, I drive better", David told her and the roar of the Ferrari covered her answer.

In spite of the hyper sportscar, David traveled within the speed limits and let himself go humming the songs that followed, interspersing the singing performances with some friendly conversation, about the weather, traffic, music.

"Hey, hey, hey!" he exclaimed at one point, turning up the volume, "Do you remember this one?! Breakfast in America!" He turned to look at her with a funny look and began to sing alternating his attention on her and on the road. He sang at the top of his lungs and clapped his hands on the steering wheel to the rhythm of the song.

Francesca laughed.

"So Franci, does it remind you of anything?"

That's how it came back to her.

Even then, September had just begun and Francesca had made an appointment with Giuliana and Sara to go to school together. A new year of high school awaited them, the third year, and although the heat was no longer oppressive, she had nevertheless dressed lightly, a little red dress, tight at the waist and a long, wide skirt. She had decided to carry the Latin vocabulary in her hands, so as not to have her backpack weigh too much and for this reason, she remembered, she walked thinking she looked like one of those fifties girls.

She and her friends were chatting cheerfully exchanging summer experiences, when a voice behind them called out her name.

"Francesca! Franci! Novelli! Hang on!"

They turned and saw him coming.

"David..." Francesca murmured cautiously. The shoemaker's son, after the summer, had grown by at least a couple of spans and now was taller than she was. The mischievous look on his face, however, hadn't changed. Indeed, he looked at her even more mischievously.

"Francesca! Girls… hi!" David adjusted his hair and stopped directly in front of her. He had some papers in his hand and waited, before continuing, scrutinizing her. It didn't escape her that he seemed to be shaking, but she attributed the reaction to running.

"Hi, David!" Sara said, moving Francesca a little so that she could stand in front of the boy.

"Ah, hi... I wanted... to tell you that... here, with my band we've organized auditions to find a singer and I was wondering if you", he looked at Francesca, "if you..."

"Oh that's great! Yes please!" Sara said taking one of the sheets. "When?"

"Tomorrow afternoon. The school allows us to use the gym and, from three onwards, if you want, you can come and do the audition. The song is the one indicated on the sheet. There is also the text, if you want... if you want... to review it."

"Okay, we'll be there, David!"

"Great!" he replied, looking at Francesca and then left as suddenly as he had arrived.

"Isn't he cute?!" exclaimed Sara dreamily.

"Mm... still a little too skinny for my taste." Francesca commented looking at the increasingly distant boy.

"Have you ever seen him shirtless, Franci?"

"No, why, have you?"

Sara's mischievous gaze struck her, as did the answer.

"I went to see him play baseball last Saturday."

"And they played shirtless?"

"No. After the game was over, I went to the locker room."

Giuliana intervened agitated: "Did you go into the boys' locker room? Are you crazy?"

"Of course not! I had him called and... well, he only came out in shorts. Eh, well, girls, what can I say? He's well built *everywhere*. And his abs... no, he is definitely no longer skinny."

"Oh my God! Saretta has fallen in love!" said Giuliana, teasing her.

"What's there not to like? He's so intriguing..."

Maybe so, but Francesca had never considered

him from that point of view. Not until then, at least. Not knowingly.

"Okay, anyway I'm not going to go at his audition."

"Oh, no, Francesca. You can't do this to me. You must come. He invited you too and I don't want to go alone."

"So then I guess I'm excused, right?" Giuliana protested.

"No, of course, not. The three of us will all go and I don't want discussions about this!" concluded Sara firmly, her gaze still lost behind David, who was no longer visible.

The following day, they had arranged to meet in front of the school gates.

Sara was dressed up as if she were going on a romantic date and Francesca adjusted her hair thanks to the reflection on one of the windows. Although her intention wasn't to impress, she certainly wasn't out to make a bad impression.

David was sitting at the drums and it was another boy who invited them on stage.

"I sing, first, then Giuli and then Franci", said Sara, imposing herself as usual.

When her turn came, Francesca sang following the advice David had given her the year before. She withdrew from everything and imagined herself a diva on the stage of an important theatre.

Her voice came out melodious and every now and then she turned to David, who was playing the drums like a demon. The understanding between them was perfect. At the end of the performance, the band gathered to deliver their verdict.

"Ehm... well, I'd say we've decided..." David began and then turned to Sara, "I think that... in short, yes, you and Giuliana sing well, but I would say that Franci..."

Sara had not allowed him to continue. "Ah, sorry David, can I talk to you?"

She took his hand and led him out of the classroom.

Since Francesca had no intention of talking to the members of the band, as Giuliana was doing instead, she followed them to go to the bathroom, but having taken a few steps, she heard Sara whispering: "... I studied singing up until two years ago and therefore I could resume and if I have to improve..."

Francesca stood around the corner eavesdropping, in disbelief at how Sara was trying hard to take her place, but as soon as David answered, she smiled.

"Yes, of course Sara... but you need charisma, like Franci... would you be ready to face the stage, the audience?"

"But wouldn't you feel better if your girlfriend was by your side?"

"But I don't have a girl-"

David stopped and Francesca, curious, looked out to understand what was happening. And he saw them. Sara was kissing David, who was wide-eyed. Maybe, Francesca thought, he didn't expect it, but his surprise didn't last long. With impetus, he encircled Sara's waist and turned her back to the wall, kissing her intensely.

At that point, Francesca decided that she had seen enough and ran away, without saying anything to her friends.

"So?" David said, pressing his foot down on the throttle and bringing her back to the present, "Do you remember? I had chosen this song for the audition..."

"Vaguely," she lied.

"That day you left without saying anything."

"You and Sara, on the other hand... she told me that, on that very day, you two got together..."

"Ah, ah, ah… you're embarrassing me… well, what do you want me to tell you. She was pretty, but it didn't last very long", he looked at her slyly, "she wasn't my type..."

"No, no, I don't want you to justify yourself... in the end those days of high school, they were good times, weren't they?"

"Well... I personally don't miss them... I wasn't very popular, in class..."

They exchanged half smiles and continuing these brief conversations, they arrived in Milan after five.

Nestled in the luxurious comfort of David's Ferrari, Francesca's heart danced with a mixture of excitement and nervous anticipation as they cruised through the vibrant streets of the fashion capital.

The city's energy surged around her, a whirlwind of sights and sounds that contrasted with the tranquility of Ravenna. As they approached Corso Magenta, Francesca's pulse quickened. She imagined the life that awaited her in this charming enclave, the possibilities and adventures that lay just beyond the threshold of her new home.

The Ferrari came to a stop, and Francesca's gaze swept over the cobblestone streets that now held a promise of new beginnings. The scent of espresso lingered in the air, mingling with the excitement that pulsed through her veins. This was her canvas, her blank page waiting to be filled with the colors of her dreams.

Stepping out of the car, Francesca couldn't help but admire the quaint church of Santa Maria delle Grazie, where the affresco of the famous Last Supper had been painted by Leonardo da Vinci during his stay in Milan.

Micaela was waiting for them in front of the 18th century building which faced the small piazza and the church of the same name. Children were playing with their mothers watching while a group of japanese tourists was diligently waiting their turn to enter the *Cenacolo*.

"Oh, great! You're here," David exclaimed satisfied. "Let's do this. Micaela, you show her the flat and see if she needs anything else, Francesca, I'll see you around eight. I'll take you out for something to eat and we'll arrange for your first day of work tomorrow morning. Does that work?"

David's smile enveloped her like a caress and had a reassuring effect. She realized that she hadn't thought of the details relating to the fact that she would have to provide for her needs in a big city like Milan, of which she knew nothing apart from the main monuments, visited as a tourist many years before.

"Thanks, David, yes, that's fine…if it's not too much trouble, for you."

"Of course not! See you later!"

"Come," Micaela said, "let me show you the place. It's on the second floor."

Climbing the staircase felt like ascending the steps of her own narrative, each stride a metaphor for the chapters of her life that had led her here. As they reached her new doorstep, a sense of pride swelled within her.

The apartment was small, but of impeccable

taste. The entrance opened onto a tiny hallway, furnished with a shoe rack and a clothes hanger, rigorously painted white, and a mirror, which entirely occupied one of the side walls, which were also white. The door to access the actual accommodation was made of colored Murano glass, sliding and retractable. It was reflected on the light brown oak parquet, which covered the entire flat.

The furniture was minimal and functional and the open kitchen was designed to integrate perfectly with the living room.

"The rollable TV is hidden beneath the floor. To make it come up, you must press this button. The bedroom is over here."

They passed a red frosted glass door. Francesca immediately liked that note of color that matched perfectly with the wood of the parquet and which constituted the perfect access to the room furnished with warm colors. A little gem of a flat that made her believe she was in a five-star hotel.

"So, the instructions for the sauna, I'll get them to you tomorrow, because I can't remember if they're here or… ah, no, here they are," Micaela said as she opened one of the drawers in the bathroom cabinet. "If something doesn't work, let me know and, if you need anything, you can call me. Let's exchange numbers."

"Thank you very much, Micaela, it was very

kind of you to come here on a Sunday."

The crease in the future colleague's mouth made her think she wasn't exactly happy, but they said goodbye politely and in the end, Francesca sat down exhausted on the soft, designer sofa, which ran across one of the walls of the living room. She relaxed. That moment felt like a rare victory from her recent circumstances and even if perhaps she had been reckless in the decision to come to Milan, she would not have missed the opportunity to take control of her life again. She was tired of being used by others. If this attempt failed, she would blame only herself. Sure she felt like a teenager chasing a white rabbit in a foreign world, but she was ready to eat any cookie. And the appetite was really there. The ringing of the intercom signaled with relief that David had returned.

"I'll wait for you downstairs," he told her.

Francesca took a look in the mirror before going downstairs. She saw a tired woman and tried to smile to rediscover a minimum cheerfulness that would help give her a better appearance.

She used the stairs instead of the elevator and found David out on the street gazing at the evening traffic.

"I still don't know how to thank you", she said. "This morning I was in Ravenna, desperate and tonight I'm in Milan..."

"You'll see that from tomorrow morning you'll

thank me less", he chuckled, "I'll take you nearby, a pizzeria. Il Nostromo... they also make other dishes."

"Pizza is perfect."

The two moved slowly, cautiously and Francesca tried to speak with indifference. "The apartment is very, very chic."

"Ah, I would hope so!" David bluntly exclaimed, "The architect I hired for the restoration, drove me crazy. The sofa in the middle of the room to give depth... the huge mirror to increase the volume... he even forced me to put that red glass door in the bedroom. He explained to me that," he mimicked the architect, "Mister Trilli, red is the color that is best perceived and in the small apartment... it serves to restore light..." he chuckled and concluded, "There was no way to make him change his mind."

"I agree with him. I actually like it very much..." she murmured and smiled.

David made a funny face and muttered: "I'm glad you like it... I'm reevaluating the architect at this point..."

The Pizzeria Nostromo was located in the newly renovated area of the Darsena, the once old dock of Milan where the two great *Navigli* canals of Milan met.

The neighborhood was busy with young people enjoying the last days of summer with their aperitivos.

Inside the pizzeria, the atmosphere felt warm and intimate. Soft lighting and vintage decor created a nostalgic ambiance, while soft jazz music added a touch of elegance to the air. Tables were set with care, adorned with candles that flickered like stars, casting a soft glow that seemed to wrap around the diners like a comforting embrace.

As they settled in, their attention was drawn to the centerpiece of the pizzeria – a traditional wood-fired oven. Its flames danced and crackled, lending an enchanting spectacle to the scene. A skilled chef crafted pizzas with precision, placing fresh ingredients atop thin, crispy dough. The sight was a feast for the eyes, promising a feast for the palate.

"It's a nice place," she said.

"I come here often. Alone."

"Oh, really? Isn't it sad? Forgive me, I didn't-"

"Actually, that's what I want. To be alone. It allows me to think. I spend a lot of time in the office and I need my own space. If I were at home, then yes, I would feel abandoned," he puffed out his cheeks in a miserable expression and Francesca laughed.

"I understand what you are saying. Lately, I've spent too much time within four walls, that, believe me, I find it hard to get back in touch with others…"

"I am not 'others'."

"No, of course you're not," she answered in a

low voice, "Indeed... I'm glad we're here, together. However," he asked the direct question: "How will this arrangement work David? Or rather, will it work? I think we both made a hasty decision this morning."

David put his fork and knife down.

"Francesca, mine was a choice taken on the fly, but not at all superficial, believe me. Indeed, you will learn, when you see me at work, I am not the type of man who decides at random. I always have my good reasons. As for whatever you think, I cannot get into your head, but please allow yourself the time to calmly evaluate whether Milan could be an alternative to Ravenna."

Their gazes didn't drop right away.

"A good speech, but you didn't quite convince me..."

"In the meantime, get ready for tomorrow morning. At nine, I set up a meeting with the staff. I'll have Gianni, our driver, pick you up at half past eight. This," he said, tapping on his cell phone, "is his phone number. Let's start here."

Francesca's cell phone lit up with David's first message.

CHAPTER 6.

The following day Francesca opened her eyes, even before the alarm rang, on a different bed from hers and with the confusion in her head due to the excited hours that had followed her assent given to David, after he had made not a very motivational speech to her, but at least one that came closer to it than anything she'd heard in the past.

Aldo, for example, had never told her that he considered her a fighter, like David did. That adjective continued to reverberate in her head and accompanied her towards her first day of work which, unlike the first day of school, would have no bell to cover the beating of her heart which was pounding fast.

David's company was nestled amidst the up and coming design district of Via Savona in Milan, David's fashion company stood as a beacon of creativity and elegance, its facade a testament to the fusion of art and commerce. The exterior exuded an air of contemporary sophistication, drawing the eye and inviting curiosity from passersby.

A sleek glass frontage framed by brushed metal accents offered a glimpse into the world within. The transparent panes acted as a window into the realm of fashion, where creativity flowed and designs were brought to life. Mannequins adorned in exquisite garments stood like sentinels, each ensemble a work of art that whispered of the company's devotion to style and craftsmanship.

The entrance, marked by polished stone steps, felt like a portal to a realm where innovation and aesthetics converged.

"The management is on the fifth floor," the driver told her, "but first you need to get your badge. Ask at the reception."

"Thank you so much, Gianni!"

The reception desk, an exquisite blend of marble and sleek metal accents, stood as the centerpiece of the room. Its clean lines and minimalist design were a testament to the company's commitment to contemporary aesthetics. A soft spotlight cast a warm illumination upon the desk, creating a focal point that drew the eye like a moth to a flame.

Behind the desk, a huge video display showcased a selection of the company's latest creations. Models draped in luxurious fabrics and innovative designs stood as silent ambassadors. Each ensemble seemed to tell a story, a narrative woven from threads of imagination and meticulous craftsmanship.

Once the identification formalities were completed, Francesca arrived at the meeting room on the fifth floor five minutes after the time indicated by David.

The room was divided from the rest of the open space by windows and therefore she stood outside the door for a moment adjusting her skirt below her knees and her hair. She let out a long breath and pushed the door hard.

Everyone turned to her, who reacted by stammering: "Sorry... good morning..."

"Francesca, there you are, come in" David, who was standing around, invited her hastily to sit in the armchair opposite him, at the head of the table, which he should have occupied. He continued towards the employees, indicating her: "Francesca Novelli... she will be my personal assistant from now on. You will have the opportunity to introduce yourself later. Now, I was saying..."

David went on and from his annoyed tone, Francesca sensed that he wasn't happy with her delay, but she didn't dare try to justify herself and sat down, keeping a religious silence. He talked, often stopping and placing his hands on the backrest and with that gesture he moved the chair backwards, continuously. Despite her opposition, keeping her feet firmly planted on the ground, it was difficult for her to resist that wave motion, but she stopped fighting that useless battle, because she noticed that everyone sitting on either side of the large table was eyeing her sideways. She concentrated on the speech.

The company was preparing for the next fashion event and David was urging them to do well. In fact, tapping his knuckles on the table, he concluded decisively: "So, this time I want you to concentrate, no hesitation. I managed to get visibility again, let's not miss the opportunity, like we did last time!"

Someone knocked on the door. It was a woman in her sixties waving a piece of paper.

"Come on in, Rosa. What is it?"

"Excuse me," said the woman entering and heading towards the boss. "Dotti called again."

David replied rudely: "So what? I'm in a meeting, can't you see?"

"I know Mr. Trilli, forgive me, but Dotti says that if you don't call him back in half an hour, he will stop production. He wants to talk to you about that matter..."

Francesca turned to look at David, who was shaking his head, puffing.

"Okay, call him back and set a precise time. I'd say," he glanced at his watch, "around noon."

"All right thank you."

"Well. Ah, Francesca, take note, then you'll see to it", David said again and Rosa leaned over her, satisfied: "Hi, Francesca... then... I'll leave you the note."

"Oh, yes, of course," she replied, seeking comfort in David, who, however, had approached the man next to her, continuing to give orders that concerned her.

"Giorgio, at this point, I would say that Francesca will take care of coordinating my personal agenda. Francesca is a person who knows the environments we are dealing with very well and therefore I want you to pass on what we have organized between now and the beginning of the fashion week. It seems to me that tonight we have dinner with Mazzanti, right?"

"Yes, but we've already indicated the names, I don't think it would be nice to change them on the go, don't you think?" the man answered angrily and David pounded on Francesca's seat. "No, fine, let's leave it at that. Giorgio, Isabella and Francesca stay. The others, back to work. Thank you."

He clapped his hands to urge those who he had ordered to leave, after which he too, went to the door and indicated to the three remaining a point beyond the window: "Put Francesca in Rosa's place, whom you will transfer to the fourth floor or where there is a free desk . Isabella, please call Gino and tell him to arrange for the transfers. From now on you and Francesca will work together. Giorgio, come, we need to finish talking about those orders." He patted him on the shoulder. Finally, he added: "Ah, one last thing. Francesca, as I told you, you report to me and to me alone."

Francesca nodded and Giorgio shook his head following David out of the meeting room.

"Ms. Novelli, I'm Isabella Bucci", the girl told her and added, "come, I'll show you the way."

"Please call me Francesca, otherwise I'll feel like your aunt..."

Isabella laughed. She was a beautiful girl with delicate features, gently plump and with a ponytail to keep her hair in order. She moved quickly and accompanied Francesca through the open space, pointing out the executive offices.

"On this floor, it's basically just Giorgio and David."

The solution of the glass partition walls, in addition to allowing the entire floor to enjoy the light coming from the large windows of the two offices, allowed Francesca to see that David and Giorgio were discussing: the former made broad gestures with his hand, while the second, from time to time, pointed a finger at her, annoyed.

"Don't worry", Isabella lowered her voice as she passed David's office, "Giorgio can be a bit arrogant sometimes, but he'll get over it. Just because he's David's right-hand man, he allows himself to argue in front of anyone about any decision David takes. He sometimes forget he isn't the boss... even if, in practice, Giorgio acts as an intermediary with the first reports, who are all on the lower floor. The HR Manager-"

"Micaela..." Francesca nodded.

"Yes, she and Alberto, the chief accountant and others you will get to know. Giorgio also takes care of legal issues as well as commercial, together with David. Instead, I mostly do secretarial work with Rosa. By the way, wait for me here. I have to tell her of the transfer."

Upon seeing Rosa, who reacted annoyed to the news of the imminent move, Francesca decided to intervene. After all, wasn't her newly appointed role as the chief of staff?

"Sorry, Isabella," she said.

"Yes?"

The two women stared at her warily.

"Ehm", she coughed to regain some tone, "Hello, Rosa, I'm Francesca Novelli. Earlier we didn't introduce ourselves properly and, if I may, in my opinion, we should call... er... Gino and have a desk brought over. For me. I think it's the best solution and I think there is enough space. It's all about understanding where it's best to put it", she turned around thoughtfully. "Will you help me?"

Rosa immediately cheered up: "Oh, yes. I agree. Thank you. Also because my desk is positioned far from the air conditioning vent and it took me years to make it clear that otherwise I'll get neck pain", she continued muttering about her state of health, but she walked away leaving Isabella to take care of her, who commented: "She's good, but she often complains."

Giorgio left David's office and walked resolutely towards Francesca.

"*Signora* Novelli", the pale green eyes did not sufficiently contrast the gray of the freshly shaved hair. He shook his head, "Once your new colleagues will create your company email account, I'll send you the links to David's calendar and mine. They must always be aligned."

"All right, Signor... Giorgio..."

The man inhaled deeply and murmured: "Giorgio Tassi."

"Thank you, Giorgio. For the patience. I think I'll need your help, at least at first."

"Er" Giorgio made a faint smile, "Yes, of course. I'm going down to get a coffee. Do you want one?"

"Thank you, maybe another time? I'd like to settle down first."

"All right. And... welcome, then", he said slightly uneasily, and then walked towards the lift.

"I'm going to get Gino and the desk," Isabella echoed, joining him.

Francesca found herself standing alone and sighed, looking around and then at David through the glass. He was busy at the computer, but he noticed her and motioned for her to enter.

She knocked lightly, "May I?"

"Come, come, Franci, close the door, please. I have to talk to you."

He clicked fast on the keyboard and occasionally looked up to observe her, irises sparkling.

The more Francesca tried to stay still, waiting, the more she kept moving like a pendulum, swaying slowly. She had never felt as lost as in that moment. Those first hours in David's company had made her realize that it wasn't going to be as easy as he had made it out to be. She bit her lip, thinking of the stupidity with which she had accepted. She took the lip balm out of her breast pocket and dabbed it quickly over her mouth.

"Everything okay?" David asked, continuing to type frantically.

"It seems to me that so far, my arrival has only created discontent," she emphasized with the click of the stick, the last word.

"Don't worry Francesca, Giorgio has his work cut out even without public relations... I'm sure that in due course, he will be happy with the new arrangement."

"I don't think so and about that…"

He spoke over her, regardless of her thoughts and Francesca got nervous.

"I'm afraid you will have to dine alone tonight."

"I'm used to it," she answered harshly. She was about to leave the office, pack her bags and get on the first train bound for Ravenna, but David carried on undaunted.

"Among other things, I won't be able to be with you for the next few days either. Unfortunately these are busy days."

Her anger was building. She cleared her throat and said sternly, "I'm not here for your… company…"

David stopped and stared at her, pursing his lips, slyly. He added in a soft voice: "And probably, on Friday… I'll go away for the weekend… unless I have to take you back to Ravenna, as we agreed…"

"David…" she tried to stop him, but the right words didn't immediately come out to start what she wanted to make appear not so much as a surrender, but as an awareness of her limits. Accepting had been a mistake and persevering would have been an aberration and a waste of time for both of them.

"This", David said in the meantime, standing up and reaching for the printer, "is the pass for a fashion show to be held this afternoon at the Piave exhibition space. I had it changed and they sent it back to me with your name. Make sure you have your company badge with you, just in case. Isabella will come with you. The show is minor, it concerns ecological fabrics, we participate with some garments, made with our fabrics, as a sample. She'll tell you more. Let's get noticed by the stylist, by the owners of the space, by the others. Public relations, in other words. Are you ready?"

David's magnetic eyes and candid smile convinced her in an instant.

"Of course I'm ready," she replied, putting aside any intention of abandoning the challenge and crushing the fears and guilt feelings that had emerged that morning in the depths of his soul.

Somehow, David sensed her upset and what he said surprised her: "Well, Franci, I'm glad you didn't give up right away, because you promised me you would hold on at least until Friday", he took her hand, "Maybe you'll find out you'll actually have fun with me."

Francesca pursed her mouth and rolled her eyes, "With the invitation to the fashion show, you almost convinced me, but with the story that you're funny, I'm almost thinking of going back to Ravenna right away..."

"Hey! I *am* funny!" David half-smiled and

squeezed her fingers.

"Do you know why I will resist this week?"

David naively denied.

He showed tenderness to Francesca and replied with a mischievous attitude, slipping the pass from her fingers: "Because, this week, thank goodness, you won't have time to entertain me! You said that!"

"Ah, ah, ah... mm... I don't know... I'm almost, thinking of freeing myself now..." he replied scratching his beard.

"If you want me to rush back to Ravenna, that's the solution. The choice is yours," she replied, and went out, turning slightly around.

She saw Isabella and went towards her, showing her the pass: "I think you'll have company for today's fashion show!"

"Oh that's great! It would have been boring to go alone. Look, Gino's busy, but he told me he'll come up with the new desk as soon as possible." She observed the floor near David's office door, "yes, it should be right here."

"Oh, well, I'll be the last stand for anyone who wants to get close to the Big Boss!" She felt someone pulling her arm. It was David.

"Francesca, after the show, please come back to the office," he raised his eyebrows and specified, "My last line of defense!"

"Yes, boss!"

The frenzy of the city was something she wasn't used to, but it was the sultry heat rising from the asphalt that slowed her down.

"Damn, my heel is sticking on the tarmac. Luckily it's September..."

"I always walk around in flat shoes. Too complicated to wear heels," Isabella suggested, showing her the way.

"Until yesterday I lived in Ravenna. Guess I'll need your advice."

"Certainly. From here we walk a little, but once we get to the square, we can take the bus and the metro. In the end, if we went by car it would take less, perhaps, but then there would be the question of parking and... poor Gianni... I'd rather do it myself", Isabella stopped, worried: "But if you want, Francesca, we can ask him to-"

"No! That's totally fine. And anyway I have to learn to extricate myself. Starting tomorrow, double set of shoes!"

The fashion show had been organized in a trendy building near Piazza Cinque Giornate and in front of the completely black steel entrance, the classic red carpet stood out. Francesca took a deep breath, because David wasn't wrong. She felt that she would have fun and this only because she found herself catapulted into her old world, and she, like the classic wolf that loses its fur, but not the vice, didn't take long to move between the canapés served at the reception and the people gathered around .

To anyone who approached her, Francesca bestowed big smiles and conversed revealing a certain competence related to fashion. On the other hand she was used to supporting events of that kind and clothes were a passion she couldn't hide.

The director of the show, Mr. Pourrin, a tall, pot-bellied Frenchman, laughed and chatted with her, occasionally raising his voice to counter the music and background buzz.

"I am very impressed by your production, my dear…"

"Oh, on the other hand, our cardigan", said Francesca, eyeing the pink garment hanging on the hanger behind them, "is soft exactly as the legendary Coco would have liked, without which today, we women, would still be slaves to pullovers , with great ruin to our hairstyles."

She had been working for a few hours at Ditali e Filati and was already able to talk about it as if she had woven that sweater herself.

"Ha, ha, ha! Madame Novelli you're right right! Your cardigan is exceptional, excellent quality. That pied de poule would please Coco, for sure. I just hope," he said almost smugly, "that your company manages to solve the various problems that have arisen lately."

Francesca stared at him for a moment, not knowing what to say or do.

When she was six, her mother often took her to visit a pair of sisters, two noble spinsters, who lived with their dogs, two beagles, and in a house all adorned in lace. One of those times, one of the sisters invited Francesca to get a candy and she unwrapped the red paper greedily. However, the taste baffled her and she was about to spit out the candy, when her mother, while calling her kindly, gave her a mean look making her desist from the intention. Not only that, she also understood that she would have to swallow that sweet lump and even say it was good.

And she did the same with Pourrin, ingesting the negative information about Ditali & Filati and confidently regurgitating a sentence that she deliberately kept generic, to avoid letting him know that David hadn't made her aware of any difficulties.

"Monsieur Pourrin, I would not call them difficulties, but opportunities. And it is clear that some slowdown is only due to the patience and love with which the activity is carried on each day. The garments we have here today are a proof of that."

"Mm... perhaps you're right Ms. Novelli, but you know, people talk..."

She quickly dismissed it: "Envy proves nothing but reality: that is, that Ditali & Filati is doing very well. If you'll excuse me now, Monsieur Pourrin. Come on, Isabella."

The girl followed her in silence and only when they were far away, in front of the drinks table, Francesca asked her: "What was that Frenchman talking about?"

Isabella sighed: "We have a problem with the workers of Cesano Boscone. Do you remember the person that called this morning?"

"Ah yes…"

"In any event, you did a great job in answering like that, David is taking care of it. He always solves everything," said Isabella dreamily.

"I guess he's a superhero uh?"

"Well, you know, David is the classic self-made man. He can be tough and assertive at times, I have to admit, but he knows the company like no other. And he is capable of doing anything. Seriously! Even the small things. I'll tell you this. Last year, the air conditioning broke down. The electrician couldn't come out to repair it for the following two days and we were trying to find another technician, but it seemed that half of Milan was grappling with the same problem. Apart from Rosa, who feels cold even in *Ferragosto*, we were all freaking out. The temperature in Milan was around 35 degrees. So David, together with Gino, sets out to fix it. I mean, the boss took a hammer and a screwdriver.

You should have seen us, it was pretty funny. Basically the two of them were working and the whole company was watching. At one point, David took his shirt off and well, what can I say, the female part of the company enjoyed the show. And what a show!"

Francesca lowered her gaze, folding her mouth and nodding. She thought that she too would have gladly given David a peek and asked her bluntly, stirring the straw in the glass: "Is he seeing anyone?"

"David? Yes... there is this woman, a foreigner, very beautiful... a model I think. He met her last year. But it is not clear what kind of relationship they have. Every now and then she shows up, especially for important occasions. It doesn't seem serious to me. He hardly ever talks about her. I don't know..."

"So she doesn't work at Ditali & Filati?"

"Oh, no, no. From what Rosa told me, David isn't really the type to mix business and feelings."

"And how is she physically? This woman, I mean..."

"Blonde and lanky, but don't worry... you'll recognize her as soon as you see her."

"Mm... okay. I guess it's time to go back at the office."

"If you don't mind, Francesca, I'm going to go home. My boyfriend is taking me out to dinner tonight. It's our anniversary."

"Oh, how romantic... Go! Run! What are you still doing here?"

Isabella giggled and added, "Yes, he's very romantic. By the way, David is supposed to have a meeting with Mazzanti, but it shouldn't last long. Basically, afterwards, he will tell you if there's anything for you to do. Tomorrow morning we go about it together."

"Okay, great! Oh and Isabella?

"Yes?"

"I wanted to thank you. Seriously. You have been very kind with me today."

"Don't mention it! See you tomorrow!"

Once back in the office, Francesca took a seat at the desk, which Gino, as promised, had placed right next to David's office entrance. The windows were obscured by the curtains, because the meeting was evidently in progress and therefore, to pass the time, she rummaged in her bag, recovering her diary. In addition to her cell phone, she liked to keep an address book, and every year she bought one with a leather cover. She had many by now and maniacally copied from one year to the next the numbers that she would continue to use. She began to write down the contacts acquired that day and Isabella's was the first.

The sound of the elevator distracted her and the doors opened on a statuesque blonde. Tall and wearing dark glasses, once she got out of the elevator, the woman moved inexorably towards David's office.

"Excuse me," Francesca, got up, going around the desk, to stop her. The height of the young woman was accentuated by the shoes with vertiginous heels and by her diva walk, which Francesca mentally defined as out of place. She tried to insist, keeping a gentle tone: "Mr. Trilli is busy in a meeting."

She put a hand on the handle, to confirm what she had just said and the woman slowly took off her glasses, saying nothing and looking at her haughtily. Slowly, she picked up her cell phone, dialed a number and rang, without taking her eyes off her.

Francesca, though embarrassed, didn't move, continuing to speak. "If you give me your name, I'll arrange an appointment for you tomorrow. Can you tell me which office you belong to?"

The blonde didn't answer her, but on the phone, annoyed said: "Honey? I'm here. There is this…lady…"

From inside David's office there was the sound of quick footsteps towards the door, which was forced open. Francesca was pulled inside and ended up falling on him.

"Gosh David, sorry!" she said holding onto his chest.

"Ah, ah, ah..." he helped her to her feet and scratched his head, embarrassed: "So the of you met."

They both stared at him dazed and while Francesca was adjusting the collar of her shirt, David said: "Katrina, this is Francesca Novelli, she works for me. Francesca, this is Katrina, my..." he faltered, "girlfriend."

CHAPTER 7.

"My first fashion show! Wow!" she exclaimed cheerfully to Isabella, who chuckled commenting: "Yes, but don't get too excited. In the end, we spin like tops and we don't have the time to enjoy the actual fashion show."

"Franci!"

David's peremptory voice called them to order.

"Uh, the boss is tense..." Francesca winked at her colleague and entered David's office, but not before taking a plastic bag with a string from the drawer. Inside was David's pass for the fashion show. She leaned against the jamb. He was intent on moving things around his desk, clearly annoyed.

"I can't find it! Damn it! Franci, do you know where-"

Francesca walked to his side and held out her hand. "Looking for this?"

"Oh," David took the bag, but she didn't let go of the string.

"The right answer would be: yes, thank you, Franci."

"Yes, thank you, Franci," he repeated smilingly.

"You gave it to me last Friday, before leaving for your long weekend. Your pass traveled too. With me, to Ravenna and back. I only trust myself."

David yanked the card towards him and Francesca took a couple of small steps forward to avoid falling. That day, she had put on her highest heels and found herself looking David almost straight in the eye. She let go of the lanyard when he asked her: "And you, Franci, how did you spend your weekend with my pass?"

"Well, I've been," she chuckled, "with an old friend. She invited me to lunch because she saw my stories on social media and that was enough to rekindle the relationship. Milan does have an appeal on people."

Isabella interrupted them: "Gianni is ready, we have to go. David, see you there?"

"Yes, wait for me outside... tonight, we'll start!"

That Friday afternoon, in fact, fifteen very important days began for Ditali & Filati. The exhibition space where they had been invited and which would have hosted the fashion show of Peter Hogen, one of their most popular stylists, was The Chapel in San Babila. A former baroque and finely frescoed chapel, the main room had been set up with two wings of chairs alongside the catwalk, arranged in a 'T' shape to allow the models to enter, pass through the guests and return to the rear rooms to the change of clothes.

David had insisted that they arrive by car and not by public transport, for a scenographic effect, so Gianni accompanied them to the front door in the company Mercedes.

The red carpet and the barriers with the golden ropes gave her the impression of being at an important gala reception and Francesca let out a deep breath when, with her twelve centimeter heels, she touched the ground.

She was finally back. After years of suffering she felt in her world again and all this thanks to David.

The roaring noise of the V8 Ferrari Roma warned them of the arrival of the boss and they waited for him at the entrance to the building. Naturally, Katrina came out of the side door. Or rather, her legs came out first. The vertiginous slit of her skirt was the protagonist of the empire-style glittery red dress she was wearing. Nothing compared to the sober tailleur Francesca wore. The skirt and the jacket cinched at the waist, over the classic white shirt. Instinctively she undid the central button and smiled at David who joined them happy and exalted: "Franci... Isabella, Giorgio... are you ready?"

"Yes, boss!"

"Good, then maybe you two could start seeing if Capitondi is around... you know him... I'd like to talk to him..."

Giorgio and Isabella disappeared into the crowd and David, waiting for Katrina, who was having a chat with some people, leaned over Francesca, with a strange look and a very hoarse voice: "I didn't tell you before , but you are very elegant, Franci..."

It didn't escape her that the boss was appreciating the cleavage more than anything else, but that compliment pleased her intimately.

Aldo rarely said nice things to her and didn't even give her certain appreciations. Convinced that she had married a moderate man, she had changed her mind the day when, by mistake, she had entered his study and while he was in the bathroom, she had seen the display open on a chat in which the serious hubby, unequivocally, had left go to lewd and indecent phrases. Reserved for another.

She pushed those nasty thoughts away and replied to David: "You are very kind, thank you."

"I really think that, and oh, try not to stray too far from me. I'll need your support later," he placed a hand on the back of her back and held it there, lightly pressed. Facing Katrina, they waited for her silently, until the blonde dragged David into the hall dedicated to the fashion show. The sensation of those vigorous fingers was still strong and Francesca observed her former classmate now turned boss with a hint of desire.

"What on earth are you thinking..." she scolded herself shaking his head.

"Come, Francesca, hurry up, it's about to start!" Isabella shouted to her from the adjoining room and she hurriedly went to take her seat.

David and Katrina had been reserved seats in the front row, while Francesca found herself behind with Isabella and Giorgio, who was feeling restless because he hadn't managed to get a front seat closer to the boss.

"I mean, that Peter... we did everything to please him, I managed to get the people of Cesano to work day and night and this is his token of appreciation? He should have reserved the entire front row for Ditali & Filati!"

"Come now Giorgio, you don't want to stand next to one of those latex dolls..." Francesca murmured in a low voice and observed Katrina. Although seated, the blonde towered over David by a few inches. Both were turned to talk to the people next to them, but they were holding hands.

A strange feeling took possession of Francesca. The sight of those fingers stretching and intertwining as the two leaned towards their respective interlocutors stung her like a sharp knife in the stomach. She realized that she wished it were her sitting next to David, that she wished she were holding those strong, gnarled fingers between hers. Those fingers that she had had on her only a few minutes before and that belonged to her by right, because of those high school years spent together.

"What a fool I'm being..." she whispered.

"Uh, what are you saying?"

"Nothing, sorry Giorgio. Maybe you are right. In fact, they could have given us a few more places, on the front row..."

A sense of unease pervaded her and she sat silently, but moving a little to continue observing those intertwined hands. She realized that her new life was changing her. Suddenly, she wanted it all, including David.

"This weekend, is David going away?" she asked, indulging the jealous movement that was building inside her. An unprecedented and overwhelming feeling for her.

"Are you kidding?!" Giorgio turned away, agitated. "And where would he go? Besides, you would be the first to know in case..."

"Oh, yes, yes, you're right... I don't know, I guess I was asking just to be sure I didn't miss anything..."

"Of course not!" Isabella added, "Imagine if

David was going anywhere this week of all weeks! He'd rather chain himself to the office!"

"Oh, right, right"

The guests took their seats, the lights went out and the fashion show began, but Francesca didn't follow the models in any way, too attentive to the boss who, in the meantime, having left Katrina, seemed intent on shaking his cell phone. Instinctively she reached into her jacket pocket and her phone vibrated.

She read the text. 'Where are you, Franci?'

She stared at the back of his neck and replied: 'I'm here, a few rows behind you.'

David turned and nodded at her, with a piercing gaze.

She reacted by waving at him, embarrassed and in the grip of those almost violent feelings of jealousy.

When the fashion show was over, he disappeared into the adjoining room, where the buffet was organised: he would have had a drink, to clear his head or to forget them.

The bar counter gleamed in the glow of the huge chandelier with crystal drops joined in an arrangement that resembled a wedding cake, hanging upside down.

She ran a hand over the marble wall and sat down on the stool, turning back at the ringing voice of

Katrina, who walked arm in arm with the stylist towards the buffet tables.

"Peter! My gosh! It was amazing!"

Once upon a time she too had been so sexy and irresistible, with clothes purchased for every occasion and often tailored to her measurements. The magic of being beautiful goes through a thousand tricks and being sensual was challenging. Once Giuliana, in a fit of envy, had reproached her that it was easy for her, that it came naturally to her, but Francesca knew it wasn't as simple as her friend thought.

From an early age her mother had trained her.

'Straight shoulders! Walk with your head held high! Look up at your interlocutors, but do not insist. Elbows close to the body! Respond politely! Never yell!' And this was all when she was still five years old.

Only after undergoing therapy following the failure of the family business to deal with the psychological wounds of going through hell did she realize that, for her mother, having a daughter with impeccable manners was a revenge to her youth made of sacrifices. Only that the price of that ransom was paid by her, not by her mother. Those haughty ways were often mistaken for arrogance and determined the relationships she had with others.

"Hey, Franci, are you alright?" David sat down

on the stool next to her and nodded to the bartender. "What can I get you?"

"A soft drink?" she answered, uncertain.

"Okay... two pesquitos, with something to nibble on, thanks," he ordered the bartender and also turned to look at Katrina.

"The pesquito is with vodka", Francesca muttered without taking her eyes off the barrel and David chuckled, justifying his choice: "Correct, but it seems to me that you need it."

She nodded and said to him with a sigh: "She is very beautiful, you are lucky."

David scratched his chin. "If you say so..."

"Oh, please don't make fun of me, I'm not in the mood."

"No, no... of course, yes, she's beautiful," he promptly replied, correcting his shot, "... she's also very spoiled-"

They were interrupted by a hoarse voice, which belonged to a fairly robust woman with an energetic manner. And that Francesca recognized immediately.

"I can not believe it! Franci! Is that you?!"

"Oh my God! Nina!"

The two women embraced passionately and Nina took Francesca's face in her hands. "Oh dear, you haven't changed at all. You are always the most beautiful! What are you doing here?"

"Oh, well, I... Nina", Francesca turned embarrassed towards David, "... I don't know if you know each other... he's my... boss. David Trilli. David, this is Nina-"

David stood up and grinned: "Nina Esti, yes, how could I not know her. I always read her articles. Lovely to meet you."

"My pleasure," said Nina, giving Francesca a curious look, evidently waiting for an explanation.

With broad nods, Francesca indicated David and tried to briefly summarize the bond between them: "Nina is a dear friend of the family, whereas David... well, he and I have known each other since high school and we met recently once again and... he offered me a job in his company."

"Yours, Mister Trilli", affirmed Nina, "is a beautiful company. I just talked about it with Annalisa Damiani, she is very happy with your partnership. She hopes to walk the same path as Peter with you. His clothes are a success also thanks to your fabrics."

Katrina was about to arrive, but David gave her a dry wave, stopping her, before answering Nina: "Yeah, let's hope so. And for us it is an honor to facilitate that path, given that Annalisa is an emerging talent..."

Katrina rolled her eyes, openly demonstrating annoyance, but sat down at a distance.

"Definitely," replied Nina, oblivious to the

quarrel between the two lovers and turned to Francesca. "Listen dear, I have to go now, but give me your number, please, because we absolutely have to meet calmly and catch up one of these days. We have many things to tell each other. After your mother left us, we never heard from each other again and this must never happen again."

"You're right, but you know... with my father's story..."

"It has nothing to do with it. Give me the number," she said hastily.

"So it's... 333..." Francesca joined the journalist, "Call me, so I can register yours."

"Unfortunately," said Nina, making the fake call and also looking at David, "the next few months will be very busy for me, but we keep in touch and organize as soon as possible. Even with you, Mister Trilli..."

David's face lit up, but Francesca intervened: "Yes, absolutely Nina, don't worry. Anyway, now I've moved here to the fashion capital and if the boss doesn't kick me out, we'll have more opportunities..." she laughed at him, which he denied with a wink.

"What are you saying, Franci..." he encircled her waist, but spoke to Nina: "Ms. Esti, we won't keep you any longer, but it was a real pleasure to meet you."

"The pleasure was all mine and, let me tell you

something, Francesca is a witty but tough girl."

"Oh, I know that very well..."

"Mm..." Nina nodded her head and hand: "So, dearest, see you soon! Until we meet again!"

As soon as the reporter was further away, Katrina joined them and immediately exclaimed annoyed: "Honey, I want to go home."

She tried to give him a kiss, but he pulled away.

"I'll have Gianni take you."

"Why?"

"I'm working, can't you see?" David picked up the phone and spoke without preamble: "Gianni... yes... can you take Katrina home? Ah yes, we are at the bar. Over here," he waved as he lifted himself up on the stool.

"At least, can I go out with John and Ella?" Katrina pressed, "Or later, do you prefer we go to dinner together?"

"No... go, have fun, don't worry about me."

Francesca tried to exclude herself from the conversation and sat down again, sipping her drink. Vodka seemed to save her, but she followed the two from the mirror, which was placed opposite, behind the counter.

"So you won't come to my house after?" She felt Katrina's furious gaze directed at her.

"No, I was thinking of going to my house.

Here is Gianni."

"Mmph… lately, you're not the same, David."

"All right," he replied absently and kissed her on the cheek, "Go, now. Bye."

The girl listlessly followed the driver and Francesca turned to David: "Look, you can go. I can hold the fort. I've got this."

"But I'm the boss, right? You said it yourself. And I can't not be here right now."

"But she is your girlfriend and it seems to me that she needs you."

"What she needs is a dinner in a nice restaurant, which she will have with her friends, and post the pictures on social networks. All at my expense. So in a way, I'm going to be very close to her. As I was telling you before Esti arrived, Katrina is very spoiled."

"Perhaps more than restaurants and jewels, she needs her man. How come you don't live with her?" The question came out insolent and with a sharp final inflection that astounded her. Her mother had taught her to be phlegmatic and not to show her emotions and her being at the mercy of this impatience annoyed her more. Being next to David made her nervous.

For his part, David, despite the impertinent question, seemed to react calmly. He took off his jacket, rolled up the sleeves of his shirt and moved the stool, sitting closer to her.

"Sorry David... this is none of my business, I shouldn't have..."

David took his glass and tapped it with hers. "Cheers..." He took a sip. "It is a rule that I gave myself right away. Never have a woman between me and my business."

"Come on, how uncompromising you are. What nonsense is this, Mister Trilli?"

"Why is it nonsense? Look at her," he raised his head pointing at Katrina, "she's happy. She has her own apartment, free meals, clothes and all the rest..."

"I remind you that there are also feelings, not just money. My my, you are a bit on the cold and cynical side... I didn't remember you like that!"

"You women generally don't even consider us, if we men don't have a minimum income. Indeed, if we really want to be precise, initially mine was not a rule, but an imposition dictated by your way of doing. When I had nothing, no one gave me credit, not even among my colleagues. Then, the bank account began to grow and suddenly I became interesting..." He clicked his tongue.

"It is not true. We women are not dazzled by money, as you say! I'm amazed you think that!"

"Oh really? So let's hear it, why when we were in high school you didn't even notice me, even though I hovered around you all the time? I'll tell you why," his tone was harsh, "Because I was the shoemaker's son, that's why! Too lame for a classy girl like you."

David's words affected her greatly. His not too veiled admission of having had a soft spot for her as an adolescent stung her in the stomach, not so much out of vanity, but because it gave her a different interpretation of those years. Of what their relationship could have been.

She rubbed her shoulder and stared at him languidly. If he intended to play with his cards exposed, why not follow the wave of emotion to which, moreover, he was already prey? Low inflection, slightly ajar gaze, she tried to speak to him openly: "Actually, David, it was you who intimidated me... you... you had... you have this amber gaze, so deep and at times imposing, with these sparkles around the iris", she moved fingers in the air, "Every time I tried to... even now... I can't stare at you... you put me in... turmoil."

She mixed the pesquito and followed the swirl of the liquid.

She sensed that the revelation had had its effect, because she felt his hazel eyes fixed on her face. She watched David in the mirror and noticed that his mouth was open, as if he wanted to say something, but couldn't speak. She saw him lean over her and turned to face him.

They had never been as interconnected as at that moment. She leaned forward and smiled at him.

David was frowning. Very serious. And also very handsome. For a moment, Francesca faltered.

She tried to be funny, to find a way out, even if her voice came out sensual: "And do you know why I'm in an uproar, David? Because today we skipped lunch and I'm hungry, very hungry... I'm afraid this aperitif has opened up my stomach."

She accompanied those words with a laugh and hoped that those unexpected confessions would get lost in the memories of the time.

David shook his head and sighed. "All right, Francesca", he stood up, paid for the drinks and put on his jacket. "Come", he said, resolutely taking her by the arm, "I'll take you to dinner..."

"Where?"

"At my house, I'll make you my award winning *Spaghetti allo scoglio*," he raised his eyebrows, sly.

"Award winning? You never cease to amaze me, Trilli..."

"Self awarded actually, I cook exclusively for the hungry Novellis of the world you see..."

Although Francesca knew she had just avoided an intimate approach, she continued to flirt with David.

"Uhm, this is tempting..."

David didn't answer, but went towards Giorgio and Isabella, gave them some instructions and returned to her, showing her the way to the garage, where the attendant handed him his Ferrari.

Francesca got into the car, her head spinning wildly. She justified herself in front of her soul: they had laughed, both were adults, they would not have crossed any line. Still, cold shivers ran up her spine. She attributed them to David's reckless driving, who entered the narrow streets of the center at a speed that was not made for urban centers. More than once Francesca had to hold on to the dashboard to avoid hitting the window.

"Ugh, I'm relieved," she said once they reached his house. "Your driving is too sporty for my taste."

"It's not me, it's her." he said indicating the car. They both laughed.

The building, in Via Brera, was entirely owned by David and the door opened onto a wonderful garden full of flowering oleanders.

"Wow…"

"Again, this the work of your architect friend… this way. I live on the top floor, the others are rented out."

They took the elevator and David pressed the button for the third floor.

The sense of guilt took over and Francesca clutched the bag she was carrying over her shoulder, muttering: "Listen, David, in my opinion, you should go to Katrina. I wouldn't feel comfortable if she found out that you made me come to your house to make me dinner, after you refused to go to her..."

"You and I need to talk."

Francesca bit her lip, noting her tense face, contracted jaws and didn't add anything else, because deep down, she was curious to understand where they were going to end up.

The elevator opened its doors directly in what was a huge open space.

Upon crossing the threshold, Francesca was greeted by a realm of shadows and light, where the twinkling cityscape outside cast its glow upon the polished hardwood floors. The open layout, now adorned with strategically placed ambient lighting, created a sense of intimacy amidst the vastness. Soft pools of light illuminated select areas, guiding the way through the living, dining, and kitchen spaces.

The living area seemed a sanctuary of tranquility, where plush textures invited one to sink into comfort.

"Have a seat," he said, throwing his jacket and tie on the velvety sofa and she advanced cautiously as if she were entering a dark den. David's virile gestures, the strong tone with which he spoke, the muscles in his chest, which suddenly seemed tense, all contributed to overwhelm her senses, fomenting the desire to be with him.

The parquet dominated everything and the windows were in an urban style, like the furniture, giving the apartment a decidedly masculine look.

It fit perfectly with David, his being a lone wolf and she felt that she was his innocent prey. And this thought excited her.

"Over there is the guest bathroom, if you need…"

She accepted that invitation, as one accepts a truce.

"Oh, yes. Thank you."

The bathroom was, in spite of what one would have imagined, very large, entirely anthracite gray with white inserts. She snooped around, opening the cabinet doors under the sink: they contained only household hygiene products and a bottle of liquid soap.

She smoothed her hair in front of the round mirror and rubbed lip balm on her lips.

She was shaking.

Being in a man's house, David's, was a feeling that she had almost forgotten and that made her feel alive again. She still couldn't get over her subtle audacity, despite the fact that Katrina was also in the picture.

She tilted her head and looked at her face. Of all the women, she knew what it meant to be the other, the abandoned one. She sighed and immediately searched her cell phone in her purse. She called a taxi and left the bathroom determined to end the evening.

At the end of the huge living room, the open kitchen spectacularly opened onto a terrace illuminated by small bulbs similar to fireflies.

"Over here!" David told her, "I already put the water on. How about we eat out?"

"David, I'm going home."

"The evening is warm enough and we can," he broke off and looked at her wildly, "what... what did you say?"

"I called a taxi. Should be here in a couple of minutes. Look, I... I prefer..."

"I don't understand, Franci."

If she didn't want any misunderstandings, in fact she had to be clear and therefore, even if she hesitated, she began to explain: "Before, at the bar... I think I involuntarily made some jokes that you could have misinterpreted... I... well... Nina said it too, I'm witty, but I don't-"

"Francesca", David leaned towards her, "I know, ours can be a complicated relationship because of our past and these... jokes, whatever you want to call them, these... teases that we exchange to make fun of each other come from our friendship. Please stay. I didn't misunderstand anything. If we're here it's because I'd like to ask you a favor. I need you to convince Nina Esti to give me an interview."

The word 'stupid' was the only one that crossed her mind. She had naively assumed that David shared her strange thoughts and felt like a fool for letting herself go like that.

"Of course, I understand", she dialed the number of the taxi company on the keypad and, staring at David, she sadly said: "Hello? I would like to cancel my reservation."

CHAPTER 8.

Less than a couple of months after the fashion event, the work had intensified and had not given anyone a moment's respite. David, together with Giorgio, was often on the road and Francesca's life practically passed between the apartment and the office. The positive note was given by the fact that the acquaintance with Isabella was intensifying and she didn't mind this, because she seemed to have found a younger sister in her.

Furthermore, Francesca had decided to take advantage of the company gym, to release the stress she had accumulated during that period. She had tried to rent a bicycle, but the streets of Milan were not like the tranquil cycle routes of Ravenna, in addition to the fact that the October days had become darker and therefore she had given up on her ambitions as a cyclist, preferring a healthy and 'safer' weightlifting.

That morning she decided to leave very early. Fortunately, the house was just behind Piazzale Baracca and the taxi station was next to the statue of the original prancing horse. That bust, placed in the center of the square, made her feel a little closer to home, because she had heard the story of the aviator since she was a child.

The Marquise Porri-Ranza had told her about it during the afternoons she organized at her home in Lugo, near Ravenna. The Marquise was the daughter-in-law of another aviator who joined the squadron of the ace of the skies, Francesco Baracca. Photos, medals, clippings from newspaper articles were arranged on display to commemorate the deeds of those heroes. Francesca was more interested in playing with the Marquise's niece, Alessandra, but she hadn't forgotten those chats between the two grandmothers.

She took the taxi and arrived at the office at half past six, said good morning to the guard at the reception and went to the gym, located on the ground floor.

The parquet was everywhere and the air conditioning was humming given that there were no windows. The room was large and a dozen treadmills, elliptical trainers and exercise bikes were arranged in a center platform, while the rest of the machines were arranged on the ground, in a circle, in an ideal path. In front of the equipment, there were two areas dedicated to weight lifting and gentle gymnastics activities and the wall opposite the entrance was completely covered in mirrors. On the right instead, another room could be seen, separated from the first by a transparent wall, inside which, specularly to the platform of the room where it was located, there was a ring and, at the back, in front of the mirrored wall, which seemed continue from the weight room, punching bags dangled.

Both rooms were empty and Francesca was relieved. She didn't intend to have conversations with anyone and immediately began her training, first dedicating herself to a light jog on one of the treadmills and later to her circuit, which the gym trainer had prepared for her the previous week.

Toning her body was the objective. At least that was what she hoped.

She sat down at the adductor machine which was placed next to the glass wall from which the boxing room could be seen. The ring was just a few meters away, separated only by the glass, and Francesca thought back to the movie Rocky. She began to train, with the music of the film's soundtrack in her head, when from the opposite side of the ring, she saw someone pass. It was the head of a man. Brown hair, wavy quiff, square jaw. She stared into the mirrors and saw the David walking confidently towards one of the punching balls. Francesca stopped lifting the weights to observe him.

After throwing his bag on the floor, David pulled on his boxing gloves. Barefoot, arms raised, red fists close to his face, he began to move back and forth in a sort of solitary ballet. Every now and then he punched the air without hitting the punching ball. He kept throwing punches and missed the mark for almost five minutes and only then did he attack the punching ball several times. He struck and dodged, striking harder again, alternately moving left and right. The red tank top underlined the shoulders forged by that type of training and Francesca continued to admire that dry and toned physique and, above all, that elegance of movement, that tense back, those rounded and masterfully finished arm muscles. David's boxing movements were an enchanting sight for her and she suddenly saw him in a different light. The skinny, insignificant boy had blossomed into a virile, handsome male. She imagined her hands caressing his body and blushed. The desire for David became urgent and to dampen her brewing inner storm, she got up suddenly. As she did so, she pushed the bar up, letting it fall back into place unaccompanied, and the weight, falling freely, slammed violently, making the classic clang. David turned around and saw her. Still flustered by her unchaste thoughts, she glanced at him briefly, grabbed her towel, and quickly headed for the locker room.

From the day she married Aldo, she had never thought of a man other than her husband in that sense, but from the moment she got closer to David, those fantasies had begun to present themselves with a certain insistence. The discomfort she felt when she was close to him was dictated exclusively by that strong attraction she felt and which she was having a hard time keeping secret. The sensation in her stomach was intense and spread all the way up to her heart.

She took a quick shower and dressed for work, trying to calm down, but her pulse increased again because, as she left the locker room, she found David leaning against the wall, evidently waiting for her to come out. He was fiddling with his boxing gloves and his hair was damp, but he'd changed out of his tank top and shorts into his standard business suit. That didn't make him any less fascinating.

"Good morning, Franci!" he greeted her cheerfully, "I didn't know you trained early in the morning, as I like to do too."

"Ah... hi... David..." Francesca stammered and added, lowering her gaze and voice, as if there were other people around, "I thought it would be good for me to start the day by exercising..."

"You're right and at this time, there's never anyone around. Typically, employees train at lunchtime or after work. Someone dares around half past seven, but there are only a few. Who wants to live such a monastic life?" He chuckled.

"You, for example, for boxing..." she replied

seriously, "I didn't know it was your passion... it used to be baseball..."

David laughed softly again and scratched the hint of stubble. "I discovered boxing when I was twenty. I needed to do something to release the tension I had built up. You know they've been difficult years... and boxing is a metaphor for life. No matter how many blows you take, you keep fighting."

"A real rampant stallion..." Francesca commented while passing him, clicking her tongue. A flush of heat ran through her, leaving her stomach for good and closing her throat, suffocating her. She wondered what was happening to her, for her feelings were a mixture of shyness and villainy, since she couldn't keep her mouth shut.

"Sorry, what? Stallion?"

'Damn!' she thought and tried to make up for what she had just said with a question: "You were born in Lugo, weren't you?"

"Yeah... you remember that too... but what does that have to do with the stallion?" His lively eyes fixed on Francesca's lips, who in the meantime replied: "Ah, you know, Rocky... the rampant horse from Lugo... I made a mess..."

She realized she was only making it worse and sighed.

"Ah, ah, ah... right... then I should call you Adriana..."

"Only if it's true love..." she gave him a sweet look and the blush on her cheeks became ardent. At that point Francesca fanned her face. "It's hot, don't you think?"

"I like that you think of me like that..." he murmured to her slyly, detaching himself from the wall and ending up on her, who backed away, thinking that the situation was definitely getting out of hand.

"Ah, David, maybe…"

"Yes, at this point, it's better to go, we have the usual briefing at nine," he said, bringing the conversation back to safe ground. However, the little smile with which he accompanied that reference to the office did not bode well for her. "Oh and tomorrow morning, we can practice together, eh? I do weights too, it will be more fun to do it in company. Shall we do at half past six?"

"Okay… fine…" she agreed, answering the phone.

"Hello? Oh hi!" she exclaimed, "How are you? How is Laura?"

Meanwhile, David led the way to the elevator as she stammered: "Ah… thank you", after which she explained to the interlocutor, "Um, no… I was talking to my boss… I'm already in the office. Ah, no, no bother. What's up?"

David continued to look at her as she spoke on

the phone and held the elevator door open for her. She hurried inside and ended the call.

"Um, yes maybe later. I have to leave you now. Yes, alright! Say hello to Laura!"

David pressed the button for the fifth floor and observed her curiously, but he didn't dare ask her anything and she let it go, also because when the doors opened they found Rosa grappling with a heated phone call.

"I told you! He's not here!" she screamed, but when she saw them, her face lit up. "Wait! There he is! He's just arrived!"

She hit the hold button hard and turned to David. "It's Dotti. He's gone mad and I can't handle him anymore! You need to talk to him."

"I don't have time..." David answered and walked into his office, slamming the door shut. Rosa stared at the door dumbfounded.

"Pass him to me, Rosa," Francesca suggested, putting down her bag and starting up the computer.

"Mm... all right but know that he's very, very angry."

She picked up the phone and nodded to her, with a resolute expression. At the other end, the man was already ranting.

"It's about time, David! How is it possible that I have to chase you like this? After all, what I ask of you is just a little of your time. And yet, many years ago, there wasn't a day that you didn't spend here. What happened? Has money gone to your head?"

Once the outburst was over, Francesca introduced herself: "Hello, I'm Francesca Novelli."

"Eh, what... who the hell are you?"

"I'm the new chief of staff and David," she made up an excuse, "has personally assigned me to speak to you. Unfortunately he is overloaded with meetings today, but he knows that this issue is important. How can I be of help?"

"Amazing... is this how David intends to help me? With a secretary?"

Those words annoyed her, but she didn't lose heart. "Are you in Cesano Boscone now?"

"Yes."

"I am coming now. Wait for me."

She ended the phone call and called Gianni. "Please, can you take me to the factory? I don't know how to get there otherwise."

"Sure, I'll wait for you downstairs."

"Rosa, I'm going to Cesano Boscone. If David looks for me, tell him to call me."

"Wait for me," said Isabella, "I'm coming too! Dotti is not an easy guy. You'll need all the help you can get."

"Okay, I guess it will be easier if you are there too, since you know each other."

On paper, the journey to the factory was

relatively short, but city traffic prevented them from arriving before eleven. That lapse of time gave Francesca the opportunity to reflect on the fact that, although her father had asked her several times to visit the factories they owned, she had always been very careful not to do so. Later, she regretted it several times. After years, she still carried on her conscience the weight of those workers who, like her, had lost everything in an instant.

This seemed to her the right occasion for a kind of *revanche*, to make up for what she hadn't done for the workers who worked for her father.

Still immersed in her thoughts, she turned to Isabella, who was drawing on her cell phone with a special pen, and commented distractedly: "Oh, wow that's gorgeous!"

"Thank you, Francesca."

"Can I see better?" she leaned more towards Isabella.

"Sure… they're just sketches… lately I've been focusing on cocktail dresses…"

"So you design clothes too?!" Francesca asked, incredulous.

"Er," Isabella blushed, but scrolled through the photos on her phone, "these are my creations. I mean I actually wish they were, but you know how it is. Sometimes dreams don't come true," she adjusted her ponytail and looked out the window. Chubby cheeks, tensed to try to hide the emotion.

"Are you telling me that you are a stylist? And that I only come to find this out now?"

The girl turned and smiled at her sweetly. "I graduated from high school and then I left my home town to come to Milan to study fashion design and pursue my dreams. The difficult part was finding a job that combined my skills and a salary. Ditali & Filati is the place that comes closest to my needs. I'm in the fashion world, after all."

"Does David know about your talent?"

"Well, not really, in the sense that he knows I graduated from the Fashion Academy, but he didn't hire me to be a designer. Oh, we're here."

Francesca took a moment to think, before getting out of the car and resolutely heading to the entrance of the Ditali & Filati warehouse. The sign was the original one, you could see it from the type of font used.

"Good morning, I'm looking for Paolo Dotti. We are Francesca Novelli", she showed her badge and pointed to his colleague, "and Isabella Buc-"

"Hello Isa!" The porter got up and walked over, straightening his trousers. His belly didn't help him and he added: "We need a gym here too!"

"Hi Gabriele! I never use the gym!"

"Eh, but you are a young girl! When I was your age I didn't need the gym either! Ah, ah, ah!" He then assumed a more formal expression, apologizing to Francesca, "Ehm, I've known Isabella for some time. Come this way. Some folks are on a break right now. I saw Paolo go into the garden, on the opposite side of where we are."

They made their way there, where a bunch of workers were chatting. Someone smoked, others ate. The porter yelled: "Paolo! People from the head office!"

A gentleman of almost sixty walked towards them.

"Francesca Novelli, pleasure to meet you."

"Paolo Dotti", he wiped his hand on his pants, before shaking it, "Hi Isabella."

"Is there an office where we can talk, Mr. Dotti?"

"I don't have a…"

"Actually," Francesca said, interrupting him, "I'd like to visit the factory. Could you be my guide?"

The textile machines produced a deafening noise, but from a certain point of view Francesca believed that that noise constituted the vitality of the company itself. Absence would have decreed its death. Just like her dad's business, Ceramiche Novelli.

"Basically this is the heart of the factory", explained Dotti, "Over there is the other room with the fabrics ready to be shipped, but this is where the transformation of the yarn takes place."

"Where the magic happens", commented Francesca and smiled.

Dotti scratched his hands and muttered, "Yes, that's right."

"What is your concern, Paolo?"

"Well, you see… the point is that we have heard that David wants to open another factory. In addition to this and to the one in Turin, it seems that he has bought a third one. Here, we all fear a decline of the business in favor of the other two locations."

"I understand," said Francesca trying to show that she knew the business plans, when in fact she knew nothing. She turned to look for Isabella's face, but she, too, seemed to be in the dark about the news. "But rest assured," she told him trying to be accommodating, "that this factory is the beating heart of Ditali & Filati."

"Well then why are we seeing our orders drop?"

The question was well posed and she didn't have a precise answer, so she tried to stay vague.

"I think the decrease is due to the acquisition of orders, which have to be rescheduled after the fashion week…"

"Is that so? Listen Francesca, the workers here are most if not all of a certain age, I won't deny it, because we go back to Fausto's times. Perhaps David is trying to save money and the new factories allow him to hire younger staff. But what should we do?"

"I'm sure David is already reorganizing to continue production at full capacity in all plants, including this one. Isabella and I will take it upon ourselves to discuss this with him."

"I hope so, because it seems to me that he invests elsewhere and not here."

Francesca gave him a deep look, nodding to underline that she understood. "I'll let you know as soon as possible, Mr. Dotti, but give me some time. Come, Isabella. Let's go. "

Returning to the exit, they met a woman pushing a large cart.

"Excuse me, what are you carrying?"

"Textile scraps," she replied, stopping and wiping her face, giving her time to observe the shreds of fabric.

"Francesca, look here!" Isabella said excitedly, "It's the same houndstooth used for the cardigan from the first show we saw together, remember?"

"Ah, yes, yes, beautiful. A softer pink than this doesn't exist," she replied and asked the woman, "Can we have this?"

"Do as you like, we throw these away, like the others."

"And why are you throwing them away?"

"Oh, for various reasons... for example, do

you see this piece? It's a test of a color that wasn't liked or the machine got stuck in it and the thread got twisted, so we had to cut..."

Isabella turned to Francesca, who proposed: "What if we take a few more samples?"

"Um, I don't know if David..." the girl replied shyly, but the woman pressed her: "Listen, if you don't want them, I'll go, I have to finish packing for the waste. Otherwise, take them even though I don't understand why you want these rags," she said to Francesca. "They are useless, don't you see?"

The woman was probably right, but Francesca was beginning to have an idea whose contours were still unclear to her, but which, she was sure, had that pile of rags in the centre.

"Actually, I don't know either, but since they will be thrown away, I prefer to take them. Isabella, take these." She put some sample tissues into her hands.

"Mm... all right, but what are we going to do with these?"

She raised her eyebrows. "Are you good at sewing?"

"It's my passion!" Isabella replied brightening up.

"Good, one of these evenings, we'll bring one of your sketches to life!"

"I can't wait! I'm starting to think about which

creation to make!"

"Me on the other hand, I already have in mind what to do with the pink pied de poule…"

Shee waved the fabric, placed it in her bag and after accompanying Isabella to the station, she returned to the office with Gianni around six in the evening. The fifth floor was completely deserted. Only David was still at his desk, making a phone call, so she began to get ready to go home.

"Where have you been?" David's question made her jump. He was leaning against the door, arms folded, and was staring at her in a gloomy, inquisitive way.

"I went to the Cesano Boscone plant to talk to Dotti. Do you remember he called this morning?"

"And what did he tell you?"

"He's worried because he fears you're ramping up production at other plants to the detriment of his own."

"Technically the plant is mine."

"Okay, yours. Dotti has been there for some time and it is clear that he has a strong sense of belonging. At least, that's what I perceived. And he also laments the fact that you don't go there like you used to."

"I happen to be busy running a business and I don't have time for everyone."

"Well, that's why you hired me, isn't it? So I

can go and talk to your employees," Francesca emphasized the adjective, her eyes widening and she continued to arrange the desk. She opened the bag to insert the agenda and a flap of pink fabric peeked out.

David took it. "This is our fabric. They make it right in Cesano."

"Yes, that's where I got it," she explained and tried to take the piece of cloth from David's hand, but he resisted.

"What are you doing?"

"It's mine," he told her.

"Not anymore, they were about to throw it away."

"You caught it before they tossed it," David's lips pursed mischievously, "so, technically, it's still mine."

"Well, technically, I need it," she mimicked him and instinctively stroked his bicep.

David shifted his gaze to her hand and Francesca removed it immediately, but he with a quick movement wrapped the piece of cloth around their palms and induced her to come closer.

"Tell me why you need it and I'll let you go," he whispered to her provocatively.

Francesca liked those amber eyes that looked at her, oh so indecently. And she also liked that body, so firm. And she felt that bold chemistry that emerged between them from time to time. It was an innocent game of looks, she thought. Perhaps. Or perhaps not. Clicking her tongue and standing up on her toes, inches from his mouth, she whispered, in an equally sensual voice: "What if I don't tell you? What are you going to do?"

"Careful, you're playing with fire Novelli," David curled his mouth into a half grin.

Francesca decided they had played enough, so she unwrapped the fabric freeing herself from his grip. "Well, I want to understand if it's possible to give it a new life. I like to sew and I would like to try making a cache-col. If you don't mind," she changed her tone and solemnly concluded, waving her hand at him, "if it pleases you, my lord of fabrics…"

"I prefer it when you call me a prancing stallion."

"Ah, ah, ah... you can be funny after all, if you apply yourself", she walked away putting the fabric back in her bag. "I also wanted to tell you that tomorrow I would like to visit the Turin plant, if it's okay with you."

"I'll take you there."

"But there's no need..."

"I insist. I'll have Isabella book us a hotel," he said picking up the phone.

"Oh no, don't disturb her, she's on the train. You know she took a few days off and is on her way home. I'll take care of it."

"Isabella? Hi."

Francesca rolled her eyes and David chuckled, before continuing to speak, "Sorry, I'm here with Francesca who's mad because I'm calling you, despite knowing you're on a train, but you know how I am… yeah. Ah, ah, ah… yes. I need a reservation for a hotel in Turin for tomorrow evening. You know the one from last time? I really liked it and if you can give me the name, then we'll do it." He raised his eyebrows at Francesca, but continued to speak to Isabella: "Uh, yes… one night. We leave tomorrow morning… yes… ah, well… then you're doing it? Otherwise… ok… ok, perfect… do I have to send you anything? Ok, yes… yes, that's fine… thank you very much. Thank you. Bye and enjoy your break."

"Of course you… you always manage to get what you want…" Francesca commented and David brushed aside: "Should I pick you up at half past seven?"

CHAPTER 9.

"Life's needs are the basis of desires, don't you see?" David was driving fast and meanwhile he was trying to convince Francesca on the subject they were discussing. "I am the example of this. Zero money, zero prospects and look at me now."

"Yes, okay, I understand, but I can guarantee you that some help is always welcome... that is, I found myself with my butt on the floor and it's not that this helped me improve."

"Instead, I believe that your desire for redemption passed right from that difficult moment. And look at you now!"

"David. If it hadn't been for you, now I don't know where I would be..."

"In Ravenna of course!"

"Ah, ah, ah... funny..."

"You said that if I apply myself I could be funny…"

"You still have a long way to go. By the way, I think the destination is right over there! Your navigator says so!"

David laughed and parked the car in front of the sliding doors of the hotel.

"Come in, Madame," he said, opening the door and handing the car keys to the concierge. "This hotel has a wonderful spa. Just what you need after a day at the factory," he smiled and turned to the receptionist, "Hi, we have a couple of reservations. One in the name of Novelli and the other, Trilli…"

"Let's see… yes, Novelli… Francesca?"

"Do you need my ID?" she asked, head bent over the purse.

"Yes please, thank you… as for, Prilli…"

"Er, no. Trilli," David interjected, "T like Turin, R like Ravenna… Trilli, not Prilli."

"Oh, I'm so sorry, I misunderstood."

They smiled at each other, not hiding the annoyance of that incomprehension, but David was surprised because the receptionist said: "I'm sorry but I can't find anything under this name."

"What do you mean?" he asked and Francesca intervened, suggesting: "Maybe the rooms have both been booked in my name? Novelli? Could you check?"

"I'll check, but I don't think so," the girl replied, raising her eyebrow.

"I'm sure it's just a mix-up, David, you'll see…"

"I'm sorry, there are no other reservations, and

the hotel is completely booked" the girl said and David looked at Francesca, saying: "What now? What do we do? I can sleep on a sofa, if there is one in your room…"

The receptionist tapped quickly on the keyboard and exclaimed beaming: "Your room, Ms. Novelli, is a double. We can join the beds if you wish…"

"Ah, no, no…" David said and clarified blushing, "…we are not married."

Francesca stared at him dumbfounded and asked the young lady: "Are you sure you have no other rooms available?"

"I'm sorry, but we are full. Tonight is the-"

David didn't wait for the explanation to finish and leaned over Francesca: "It's late now and we won't be able to find an extra room. Guess we'll have to settle… what do you say? Personally, I need to take a shower and would also like to have time to use the spa, so we could split up. I go to the spa and you occupy the room. This way everyone will have their own space. And to sleep… well, it won't be the first time you've slept in a room with a man, will it?"

David's words touched her like soft silk and instinctively she moved closer to him.

"Franci... is it okay?"

She sighed and moved away stating seriously: "I'm okay with it, but I'm coming to the spa too."

"Good idea. You will like it."

The spa had a colorful ambiance due to the use of floral majolica tiles in blue and yellow tones, which covered the walls and a fake well, placed in the center of the room. Instead of water, the well contained pink salt.

"This well is beautiful! Look at these tiles!" Francesca rushed like a child to touch the tiles that decorated it. "You know", she turned to look for David, apologizing for that euphoria, "I inherited the passion for tiles from my father..."

"I like this passion of yours, it enlightens you…"

"In Ravenna," she continued smiling, "along the Fiumi Uniti there is a farmhouse with a well, more or less like this one. Every now and then I pass by on my bicycle and stop to admire it. I would like to live there and decorate the well with the majolica left over from the bankruptcy of my dad's company…"

"And maybe we could put a hammock near it", added David, "And be together to look at the sky above and the stars..."

"Oh," Francesca turned and stared at David who was scooping up the salt with both hands and slowly dropping it again. "I didn't think you were so romantic..."

David just smiled at her. "No, in fact, I'm not.

I'm going to take a dip in the pool."

They remained apart, each relaxing at a distance, he swimming and she in one of the two small jacuzzis. However, their gazes did not stop scrutinizing each other and when they returned to the room, they hesitated for a moment.

"Where do you prefer to sleep?"

"On that one, if you don't mind," Francesca replied, pointing to the bed by the window and the bathroom.

"Well, you do it first, then", he pointed the bathroom and she, after taking what she needed, gently closed the door, emphasizing the discomfort, which was also caused by the usual strange thoughts that crossed her mind. She looked in the mirror and saw the first wrinkles at the corners of her eyes which suddenly appeared more pronounced.

She hadn't slept with a man since Aldo left her and David was indeed a Man with a capital M.

"Besides the fact that he's already taken," she admonished herself to divert attention to David. She took off her bathing suit, put on her nightgown and sighed, pulling on her bathrobe.

She went out and made her way to the bed, avoiding looking at him. Quickly, she took off her bathrobe, placed it at the foot of the bed and slipped under the covers, leaving her face uncovered.

David passed her saying ambiguously: "You

know, I must confess that I generally don't wear pajamas... so don't look", he barely opened the door and reopened it immediately afterwards.

"David don't play jokes, huh?! You won't be adamic, I hope!" she said, taking a finger away from her face and eyeing him sideways.

"Ah, ah... so you are curious after all, Novelli..." David laughed and moved the covers off his bed, throwing them on the floor. He only held the sheet, but did not cover himself and added: "I told you not to look... anyway, for your sake, I'm wearing boxers."

"You're weird... who knows how your girlfriend copes with you..."

"Meaning what?" David ruffled his hair.

"Well, you don't cover yourself, you sleep naked... the two of us could never share the same bed, that's for sure!"

She turned purple and her embarrassment increased, because she realized that he was staring at her ironically.

"Mm… what are these thoughts, Novelli? You surprise me…"

"I meant that I like being wrapped up in blankets because I'm always cold while you throw them away... it was just for... what did you think I meant?"

The clucking with which David accompanied

the mischievous glare helped to make Francesca blush even more.

"Uff, David, turn off the lights!" she muttered, rolling onto her side.

"Alright, goodnight then…"

"Sorry! Can you turn it back on?"

"What is it?" David stood up and she took the bag. "I can't sleep if I don't put cocoa butter on my lips and I forgot…"

"Ah…" he murmured, putting his hands behind his head and carefully following her moves.

"Uff…" Francesca muttered, passing the stick, "… it's almost finished and I forgot to buy it. How annoying!" her eyes goggled and David chuckled. "You're funny, Franci."

"And you are no comfort at all, you cannot understand, I can't live without lip balm. All right", she dived under the covers and gave him one last look, "Goodnight, David!"

"'Night, Franci..." he answered affectionately, turning off the lights for good.

However, the light did not diminish and Francesca turned, staring at the door. Someone was knocking insistently. She went to open it and strangely she didn't find anyone. She checked the corridor, which, at first, seemed empty. Only after a while did she become aware of a figure at the end of the corridor, who was running towards the stairs. She decided to follow him, but with each step the lights went out. When she reached the corner, it was completely dark. She tried to go back and realized that she would no longer be able to orient herself. Panic gripped her, so she started to go down the steps, carefully. It was then that Aldo appeared, with a fearful grin on his face. She stepped forward and he purposely tripped her. She tried to hold on to the railing, but it was impossible. She fell into the void.

"Aargh!"

The scream woke him up with a start, but he reacted lucidly. With a leap he was at Francesca's side. She was wriggling and moaning. David knew he couldn't wake her abruptly, but he would have to indulge her by preventing her from getting hurt. In fact, she was pulling her hair and scratching her chest, as if she wanted to get something off her back.

"Shh..." he began to whisper and stopped her wrists, pushing her arms back at her face, but Francesca continued to move her head like a possessed person. Then, he approached and lightly pressed his body on hers: "Shh..." he continued to whisper in a rhythmic buzz and she slowly woke up.

"David…"

"Shh…"

"Oh God, sorry… I had one of my usual nightmares…"

"It's all right, Franci..." he said, lying down

next to her and gently leaving her arms.

"I was falling… and…"

He stroked her face, her hair: "I got you, Franci. I'm here, now", he squeezed her in a tender hug, "Go back to sleep…"

Francesca nodded and looked at David's eyes illuminated by the first flashes of a new day. The color of the amber reminded her of honey and she drank the nectar of that mighty divine being who had saved her, calming down and falling asleep again.

This time they huddled together, close.

What woke her later was the weight of David's body resting on hers. He had placed a leg on her stomach, an arm on her chest and with the fingers of the one he kept under his head, every now and then, he stroked her hair.

Francesca turned slightly to see his face. He had his eyes closed and a blissful expression. His perfume intoxicated her and knowing that David was basking on her excited her.

"Are you awake?"

Amazed that he had noticed, she replied with a shy nod. David's leg pressed more on the covers and began to caress her neck, going down to the hollow of her breasts, with an indifferent gesture.

"Do you mind if we stay like this a little longer, Franci? I am having profitable thoughts…"

"Can I ask about what?"

"Work of course," David replied softly, but added, "I'm looking for a new company name. Ditali & Filati, I'd say it's had its day..."

"I like it... but it's true. I think acronyms are more fashionable now. You could call it D&F," she stammered, "Like... our... initials, David and... Francesca. Although if you look carefully it would not be immediately understandable what the company does, unless-"

"What did you say?" David leaned completely on top of her and stared at her. The amber moved probing Francesca's eyes and gave her the impression that he was piercing her soul. The weight of the sculpted body accentuated that perception.

Awkward, she replied, "I said you should pick a name that immediately conveys the idea of what you do-"

"No. Before."

"Um, that you could use the initials... Ditali and Filati D and F..." she added, laughing like a little girl, "like mine and yours."

"D and F. Like Dorina and Fausto. That's why he didn't want to change! You are a genius!" he planted a kiss on her cheek and reached out for his cell phone.

"Really... I don't understand..."

"That's because you're a genius!"

"Putting it that way, it might be offensive,

David. You're not funny..."

He laughed and spoke on the phone: "Hello? Isabella? Hi, sorry for bothering you again, but I urgently need to talk to Giorgio and Elena, find them and call me back. I'll be waiting."

He adjusted his elbows better and began to smooth down a ringlet. "What do you say? Do we use the ampersand? Or shall we put the dots?"

The phone rang and Francesca didn't have time to reply, but David didn't abandon his position and asked her to answer: "You take your cell phone and put it on speakerphone, please." He continued to brush against her, his lips pursed slightly in a hermetic smile for Francesca, which he carried out, holding the cell phone in David's favor.

"Isabella? Are you all there?"

"Yes, I called Giorgio and Elena, as you asked."

"Well. I decided to rename the company to D & F, so Giorgio will need to prepare everything for the bureaucratic aspects, but, first, Elena will need to hire a company that deals with corporate brand design. I still don't know if I want to call it only with initials, with dots or what else. I want some proposals, also for the logos and while you're at it give me a timeline and the costs. Send everything to Isabella. Isa, arrange a meeting right now for when you get back."

"Okay, it will be done!" the girl exclaimed.

Francesca pressed the red button and slid the cell phone aside.

She looked back at David, who sank dangerously towards her lips, his body tense and trembling, until his mouth was delicately placed just above her chin. The breaths became slow and both were amazed at that tingling that drove them to press against each other, towards each other.

It seemed to Francesca that David's eyes were brighter, perhaps because of the sunlight that crept through the curtains.

She moved her lips rubbing lightly on his and his taste stunned her, like an enveloping fragrance. She stroked the strong muscles in his shoulders and fretted at what he was about to say.

He made an effort, to try to savor and keep in memory that instant, before ruining the magic, with a whisper: "David... I don't think it's a good idea... your fiancée..."

He stared at her uncertainly, but finally, he broke away, standing abruptly. Francesca followed him with her languid gaze, appreciating his back, his body, so marble.

"Sorry, Francesca... I'm euphoric, I didn't want to... that is, well... I'm going to take a shower", and he specified, "a very cold shower..."

She let out a soft chuckle and pulled the

covers up to her chin. She still felt David's physique overbearing her in every point and she wanted him, she wanted him ardently, but she was aware that she wasn't ready to compete with the sexy model with which he accompanied himself. And she certainly didn't want to be treated like a whim that David could indulge at will. Sure, she too could have considered it a mere whim, but the way she was, she knew that guilt would prevail, possibly undermining her professional relationship with him.

She dressed quickly and sat down to wait for him, placating her feelings.

When David came out of the bathroom, wearing a jacket and tie, Francesca's cell phone rang.

"Michele from Laura..." David murmured as he took the phone. "Well, whoever he is, now you don't have time for him, only for your boss. I'm hungry, let's go have breakfast."

"A grumpy boss, apparently…"

"Grumpy, but definitely more interesting than this guy," he handed her the phone and smiled.

CHAPTER 10.

"Can't you just walk over to my place?"

"Honey, I can walk over tp your place but my luggage can't. Besides, you don't want me to go out alone so early in the day, do you?"

"Alright, alright. I'll come and pick you up," David agreed, because, although bored by that request, he was aware that Katrina was absolutely right and his was a clumsy attempt to ruin the Christmas vacation they had planned before the summer and were about to embark on. Instinctively, he would have wanted to cancel everything, postpone, avoid, do anything to not go.

"Thank you! Ah, David, remember sunscreen…"

"Huh? What?!"

"The…sunscreen."

"Uh… yeah, yeah, sure."

"Ok! Love you."

"See you tomorrow." He closed the phone call, the suitcase and threw himself on the bed. Gaze fixed on the ceiling for almost the whole night, so much so that when Gianni buzzed the intercom, early in the morning, he had already been ready for at least an hour.

"Is she in the car?" he asked the driver.

"Um… yes, she is Mister Trilli."

"Good. I'll be down in a minute," he answered, opening the door and sighing. The question had come out spontaneously, but the answer was not the one he had hoped for. He had imagined a hitch, an external impediment that would have resolved the matter in his favor. But instead she was there.

"Hello, Katrina…" he said as he got into the car.

"David."

They kissed on the lips, without passion and both got on the cell phone, Katrina ticked frantically, with her long, red-lacquered fingernails, while David raised the device to his ear, waiting for someone on the other end to answer his call.

"Hello, Franci?"

"David? Hi. Weren't you supposed to leave?"

"Ah yes, we are going to the airport."

"Oh good. Do you need something? Today I'm in the office all day, so…"

"No, I… I wanted to know if you sent the email to Torrini."

"Yes, already done. I thought I copied you, wait let me check."

"No need," he instinctively turned to Katrina, who continued texting regardless of what he was saying.

"Are you leaving tomorrow for Ravenna?"

"Yes, I have the train at nine."

"Are you going alone?"

Francesca stared at the receiver, as if this would help her understand the question better and resolved to say: "Well, yes..."

"I'll have Gianni take you."

"David... no. From the Conciliazione tube station to Centrale it takes five minutes max."

"But tomorrow is the twenty-fourth of December..."

"So what?"

"I insist. And I mean Gianni will take you all the way to Ravenna."

"Are you crazy?! That poor Gianni has a family to think about. Thank you for this fraternal interest but honestly-"

"It's not fraternal."

"Okay paternal."

"Stop it, Franci", David said annoyed, "It's not a problem for Gianni, he's used to-"

"No, you stop it, David! I've already organized everything. I don't need your help. I know that with the nightmare story, I may have given you the idea of fragility, but during the day," she chuckled, "I am strong and able to take care of myself… seriously…"

David sighed. "Uff... all right..."

"Just try to relax and enjoy your vacation okay? I'll see you when you come back."

"Ah… yeah… but… you… work after Christmas, right?"

"Of course, as agreed. Among other things, this afternoon, I'll meet with Nina to wish her well and I don't know, she told me she has to tell me something, maybe it's for the interview, hopefully... let's see."

"Fine, then I'll talk to you later."

"I'll write you in case of important news."

"No. I'll call you anyway." He pressed the red button, but held the phone to his chin, rubbing his beard up and down thoughtfully, looking out the window.

That woman was like the devil for him, but not in an evil way, but rather as a captivating and crazy Lilith for how she managed to attract him and make him vulnerable. For someone like him, used to being in control, to having full dominion of the relationships he embarked on, he felt that for the first time he was giving away pieces of his soul. And he wasn't happy of that.

The flight to Mauritius was scheduled for nine and they would arrive around ten in the evening local time, but the first class stewardess warned them of a delay, inviting them to relax in the lounge.

"Things should be fixed shortly. Would you like something to drink in the meantime?"

"Um, no… thanks", he took his book, a legal thriller, and opened the pages listlessly. Only two minutes passed and he closed it again. He placed a hand on Katrina's leg, who was listening to music, and walked over.

"Everything okay?"

"Yes, honey," Katrina took off her headphones and ran her forefinger, with her maniacally manicured nail, up her chin. "How about you?"

Katrina's Italian improved every day, but the foreign inflection persisted. He liked those slurred words, they were nice and made him smile. That day, however, did not have the usual effect.

"Mm… well… I'm tired."

"Why don'y you close your eyes a bit? I'll wake you up when we need to board."

"Mm… yeah, good idea."

"Hey," Katrina shook his arm. "Before you fall asleep, listen to this song. What does it remind you of?" She didn't wait and put the headphones on his head, winking at his memory.

David looked back at her and tried to remember, but nothing came to mind and she, taking back her headphones, blurted out annoyed: "The first time you met me, last year, at the Palazzo delle

Stelline, I was listening to this song, Paradise."

"Oh yes, that's right." He leaned towards her and gave her a light kiss on the chin. "A beautiful song," he murmured and lay down, arms folded. He evaded eye contact, but out of the corner of his eye he saw that Katrina was not satisfied with his answer.

The day he had met her he had been struck by her beauty. In particular, by her long, silky legs. He had been invited to a conference and when the elevator opened to the floor, Katrina was standing in front of him, wearing a skimpy dress that sparkled with sequins. Katrina had smiled at him, handing him his badge and he had asked her what she was listening to. Evidently that song, which he didn't remember now. They had sex that same night, in his office, on the conference table, and their relationship took off.

Strange that he didn't remember Coldplay's Paradise, because he was a music lover and every important moment in his life had been tied to a song.

'Com'è profondo il mare', the song by Lucio Dalla, reminded him of the day his grandfather took him fishing on the Reno for the first time. Or Catfish, by Bob Dylan when coach Anderson, who came specially from the United States to teach the course summer baseball, told him he was a good catcher. And also Shattered Dreams, by Johnny Hates Jazz, linked to the first kiss, chaste, even before the real one received in high school, and which had been bestowed on him by a middle school classmate. He smiled, thinking back to that episode. In that instant, suddenly and unexpectedly, he understood that females were a mysterious and fascinating world in which he wanted to become an expert.

And then of course there was 'The Song'. The one with a capital S. The one he often hummed, that it was enough for him to listen to, to get back in a good mood, the one that reminded him of her. And that since September, it was once again fixed in his head like a woodworm that enjoys moving from one lobe to another, sometimes presenting itself only with the rhythm, at times forcing him to sing the words.

Breakfast in America, by Supertramp.

A music that was a trap, a net, in which, after all, he liked being entangled into. And this also happened once they boarded the plane. The song continued playing in his mind, not allowing him to sleep.

The resort in Mauritius had sent a limousine to pick them up and during the journey from the airport to the hotel David dared to write to Francesca, even though it was almost past midnight.

'Hi. I just landed and I didn't manage to call you in time. We will talk tomorrow.'

He hit the send button and read the message again. He huffed because he never stooped to justify himself to an employee.

"Damn it…" he muttered to himself.

"Honey?"

The message had been sent and deleting it would have been worse. There was no alternative but to stop thinking about her. He hugged Katrina and the cell phone rang. He answered without looking.

"Hello?"

"Hi, David, it's me."

He broke away from Katrina and moved forward. On guard. "Franci, hello, sorry, I didn't want to disturb you..."

"No trouble. I was waiting for your call."

He touched his beard in response, but the words didn't come out. "Um…"

"You said you would call me and so when I read the text…"

Francesca's voice was warm, sensual and David imagined her in bed, under the covers.

Naked.

"I hadn't thought about the time and the delay with the flight... tomorrow you also have to leave..."

'Good heavens,' he thought again, because his words seemed too cloying.

"It doesn't matter", Francesca's voice was even more sensual, "I'll sleep on the train and also... I wanted to tell you right away. Nina has decided she's going to write an article on you, Ditali & Filati, and the employees. Four or five pages, photos, editorial, everything... I'll meet her next week to start putting down some questions. And, hold on tight, she told me that she has already sold the exclusive to one of the major national newspapers. She didn't want to tell me which one, but... well, it's fantastic, don't you think? You know that she is considered by everyone..."

Francesca's words mixed with the images that were blurring his vision and confusing his mind. He fantasized about getting her on a bed, pulling the covers away, caressing her slowly and making love to her. Passionately.

"... well, in the end, in my opinion, even in terms of timing, it's perfect, right? David?"

"Er, yes... whatever you decide is fine with me..."

"Oh, no, no! With Nina you decide what she decides!" Francesca exploded in a scratched, low laugh and David wanted to hold her, take her neck, kiss her behind the ear and then kiss her all over. He became excited and shifted in the seat.

"Okay, enough work, I'll leave you to your holiday then. Say hello to Katrina for me."

David was silent for a moment. He wanted to say something to her, he didn't even know what, and he folded his mouth in frustration: "Ok, maybe we'll talk later, if... if you need me."

"No, boss! Enjoy your holiday, it's an order!"

This time it was Francesca who ended the call.

"Who was it?" Katrina asked as she got out of the car.

"A colleague… I… asked her… to advise me on an important matter."

"Okay. Come, let's go to the room," she replied. She hugged him and kissed him.

"Mm… yeah…" David babbled, thinking that was what he needed. The candid white sheets of the room were waiting for him to fully satisfy his desire. He pushed Katrina onto the bed and took off his belt.

"Oh my…" she said helping him unzip. "It's big…"

"And bad…", he answered slyly.

"Come here, you bad boy, you…"

He slipped off her panties and stroked her thigh as he leaned over her. He caught a whiff of vanilla, which made him turn his head.

"Honey…what's wrong?" Katrina muttered, grabbing his chin and pulling him back to her.

"Ah, sorry, I thought… I heard… nothing. Where were we?"

He kissed her, but he realized that his body was looking for the body of Francesca. He closed his eyes and imagined himself with her. The curls, the French nose, the pucker at the corner of her mouth, which was accentuated when she laughed.

He narrowed his eyes and saw Katrina.

He returned to his imagination and stroked his

princess's full breasts. At the class reunion, his senses had given him an accurate representation of how she was made, of how her breasts were firmer than when they were teenagers.

He bent down to kiss Katrina's breasts and spread her legs, thrusting in.

"Oh yes, David!"

His eyes widened. The princess was not there and in her place Katrina caressed his head and shoulders debauchedly.

He tried to commit himself, because he was objectively excited, but his daydreams, instead of helping him, prevented him from letting go. They kissed and caressed for a long while longer, until he rolled over to the side, belly up, staring at the ceiling.

It was Katrina who spoke: "I'm sorry sweetie. Maybe you're tired. I'm sleepy myself. The journey took too long."

The days immediately following were cadenced by lunches and dinners organized to ensure that the guests of the resort could celebrate Christmas, cheered by the shows organized by the hotel while David kept his distance from Katrina with the excuse of a mild illness.

Finally one morning he joined her intending to stay closer to her and try to forget Francesca.

"Can you put some sunscreen on me honey? I've finished mine."

"Uh, sure, which one?"

"Oh, I don't know what protection did you bring?"

"No… I mean I don't have any sunscreen…I forgot to bring it."

"David! Seriously?!" Katrina reacted angrily. "I told you at least fifteen times. Oh, my god! You are so… so… aw forget it! I'm going to go buy it."

"Yes, sorry, just put it on the room."

"Obviously!" She left with her slouching gait and when she returned, she moved the bed away from the one where he was sipping a drink, admiring the private beach, the white sand, the turquoise lagoon. He watched Katrina carefully apply the cream all over her body. Especially on the legs. David knew he could get up, walk over to her and ask her to do anything. And that she would satisfy him.

Yet he would not be happy.

He got up and went to the gym. He needed to let out some steam.

Luckily the room and equipment were completely facing the ocean and the view calmed him down. He got on the treadmill and started running, looking now at the shore, now at the wooden platform that crossed the area in front of the gym's windows.

A couple walked past, slowly. The woman, with long black hair, tanned, carried a little girl with golden curls in her arms, while the man, massive and imposing, taller than her by at least fifteen centimeters, carried a little boy with a black tuft on his shoulders. The man was objectively handsome, similar to a Greek god and, according to his tastes, she was pretty too, but the man could have aspired to someone more beautiful. The woman turned her gaze towards the window of the gym and then David understood why the man had chosen her. Such an intriguing look, he hadn't seen often. It had only happened to him with one woman, the only one who had made his heart stop. And when it started beating again, his chest had hurt badly.

The two were no doubt arguing. He understood this because of the withering looks she threw at the Greek god. David would not have wanted to be in the shoes of that poor man, who bent down repeatedly, looking for a contact that the woman did not intend to grant. Glacial, was the adjective that David attributed to her, slowing down the pace of the machine, to better follow the altercation and the two, not even on purpose, stopped right in front of where he was.

The man let the child down and the woman did the same with the little girl. The children then ran happily towards the ocean, while the parents continued to argue. The woman had her arms folded and the man gestured, adjusting his hair from time to time.

And finally, what David thought was magic happened.

The woman rose to her toes, still a deadly gaze, but giving her husband a break. It consisted of a kiss. Tender, bestowed on the chin. She was lowering herself again, but the Greek god grabbed her and wrapped her around him, lifting her and kissing her as if time had stopped, as if there were only the two of them in the whole world.

When they parted, called back by the children who were returning, the storm had passed on their faces and their hands did not detach, not even when the children wanted to return to their arms.

David wasn't the type of man susceptible to romance, but those two left him with such a craving for sweetness that he struggled to tame it. Subdued by that urgent need, he took the towel, put it around his neck and went to the beach, to the exact point where those two had kissed. He wanted to feel the love around him as he got ready to compose the message.

'Good morning. I hope you're awake… I just wanted to know how you were. If you had a good holiday and… nothing. That's all.'

He crossed out the word 'nothing'. And then he deleted the entire text.

He sighed and looked at the little family by the sea. The Greek god was making the children play in the water and the woman was lying in the sun on the shoreline. Every now and then the god dropped by to find the mortal, to see if she was all right. Evidently, she was fine, because she revived thanks to the kisses bestowed by the colossus.

He went back to thinking about the type of message to send. He inhaled and immediately wrote: 'Hi Francesca, I hope you had a good holiday.'

"Damn..." he whispered and deleted the message he had just typed again.

'Hello Francesca. Have you had any other bad dreams?'

He pressed the enter key and stared at the display.

"Stupid! Stupid!" he tapped his cell phone on his chin, and it vibrated.

He returned to staring at the display.

Francesca had replied.

'Hi, David. No, fortunately not. You are very kind to ask me. How are you? How is the vacation going? I have been to Mauritius years ago and it was really beautiful, especially the Pointe de Flacq beach at sunset. Very, very romantic.'

David smiled at that last adjective used by Francesca, who had unknowingly struck a chord that was playing loudly inside him.

'Yeah... very romantic... What are you going to do today?'

'Oh, today I will still be in Ravenna and after

spending the last two days with my family (I can guarantee you that I was sick of it!) I will finally see my friends. They organize an afternoon of naughty card games.'

'Hey! What do you mean, naughty?'

'Ha, ha, ha, in the sense that we play for money! And since I'm unlucky in love… hopefully I'll be lucky at gambling! And what about you?'

'You know the usual stuff, swim, drinks…'

'Oh, poor thing… I can only dream of a holiday like that these days…'

He sent her a smiley face to which she responded with an angry smiley. He wanted to continue, but saw Katrina approaching.

'I have to go, Franci, but, if it's all right with you, I'd like to write to you sometime…'

David clicked the send button and raised his face, aware that he had used words from other times yet completely right. And he had confirmation of it, as Francesca's response was not immediate.

'Yes, of course, I would really appreciate it if you wrote to me sometime.'

David perceived her embarrassment and surprise between the words and was sure he had hit the mark. And once Katrina arrived and stood a few yards away, beach bag over her shoulder, he'd already made up his mind.

"Honey, I'm going for a massage. All right?"

"Yes, of course... ah, Katrina, listen, I have to go back to Italy", he waved his cell phone, "an urgent commitment emerged, but you can stay of course."

He felt like a worm, but he had no other choice, he couldn't lie to himself anymore and as charming as she was, he had to go to his personal goddess of love.

"I understand. And when are you leaving?" Katrina asked and pushed her glasses aside slightly, moving her face slowly.

"The time to pack my bags."

"And... when I come back to Milan, will you be there?"

The question was trivial, but David bit his lip. It was enough for Katrina to understand and with frozen eyes and an altered voice she walked away, saying: "You are an asshole!"

David didn't catch every word perfectly, but the meaning, that one, came through loud and clear and although he was sorry he knew there was no other way. He had to go to her. To the woman he loved.

He started running. He ran to go back to her room to pack his bags, he ran to go to the airport and he ran to get to Milan, as if that frenzy would have contributed to decreasing the time distance necessary to reach Francesca.

On the Malpensa Express and on the subway he stood, jerking one leg spasmodically, agitated. He imagined the meeting, but could not outline what he would say to win her over. As soon as the doors opened, he headed for the exit and climbed the steps, which separated him from Corso Magenta, in twos and twos.

He knew he had a stupid smile on his face, he couldn't stop smiling. The smile of someone who is about to do something crazy. The smile of someone in love.

His mad rush, which lasted a couple of days, ended a few meters from Francesca's door.

She was there in front of the building in Madonna delle Grazie.

In the company of a man.

David blinked to make sure he was seeing correctly and examined the man. In his fifties, maybe less, balding and judging by the tight jacket, with a pronounced belly. He held a bag in his hand and chatted amiably with her, who laughed.

"Who is this asshole?" David babbled, backing away a few steps.

Francesca's cell phone rang and she, to answer, moved to the small piazza, not far from where he was. He hid behind the billboard of the tram stop and continued to observe. He heard her answer, "Hi Nina! But no, no, no trouble. Imagine... sure... oh, perfect! I'm working tomorrow... oh, sure... yes... all right, see you tomorrow then! Thank you Nina!"

Francesca continued to turn her back on the man she was with. She started to put her cell phone in her purse, but hesitated and held it to her ear. She took out her diary, returning to the door, saying, in a ringing tone, "Sure, let's do it at eight... Nina, can you wait, please?"

The distance was such that David could not understand what Francesca was saying to the man, but from the latter's face, he understood that she was about to dismiss him.

"Well, good girl", he murmured satisfied and was much more so when the man handed the bag to Francesca. They saluted each other with a kiss on the cheek. And then another, on the opposite side.

"Even the third one... what the fuck, Franci..." David commented and jealousy twisted his stomach, but he didn't move. Francesca meanwhile walked towards the entrance of the building, continued talking on her cell phone and put the key in the lock, with some difficulty because of everything she had in her hands.

"Go away..." David urged, addressing the command to the man, who seemed to hesitate, but who finally, saying goodbye to Francesca again, disappeared around the corner. "Yes, go, leave already!"

Francesca took a step back as if to make sure

she was alone, then slipped her cell phone and diary into her purse, opened the door and disappeared from David's sight.

He slipped his hands into the large pockets of his jacket and walked in the direction of the Duomo to clear his head.

With a series of melancholy love songs in his head, he sensed that a busy night was looming for him, but different from how he had imagined it. A little pink and very exploded night. And he let passion dominate his thoughts. And he concluded that he certainly would not give up on Francesca. Not now, not ever.

CHAPTER 11.

In the heart of a crisp January day, Francesca found solace at a cafe in Piazza del Duomo, Milan's beating heart. Clutching a warm cup of espresso in her gloved hands, she relished the steam that rose in delicate swirls, the aromatic fragrance mingling with the chill of the winter air. The bustling piazza seemed to hush in reverence to the season, embracing a quieter rhythm beneath the pale winter sun.

Before her, the Milan Cathedral, the majestic Duomo, stood resolute against the cold. Its spires reached skyward, adorned with a delicate dusting of snow that added an ethereal charm to the intricate details of its architecture. Francesca's gaze traced the frost-kissed contours, a testament to the enduring beauty that graced this city.

Around her, life continued its dance despite the chill. Couples walked arm in arm, their breath visible in the crisp air as they shared whispered conversations. Tourists donned scarves and hats, their faces alive with wonder as they captured the Duomo's grandeur through the lens of their cameras. Children bundled up in colorful jackets played with pigeons, their laughter echoing like chimes in the winter breeze.

In this timeless corner of Milan, Francesca felt a sense of serenity settle over her. This new, unexpected chapter in her life had brought her many new things. A well-paid job, an apartment in the center of Milan, old friends and, above all, a smile. The latter mainly due to one person: David.

During the Christmas holidays they had exchanged a few messages and although he had promised to write to her, in the end he hadn't been heard from again. Obviously, Francesca had let it go, because David's silence, on the other hand, was understandable, given that he was on vacation with his girlfriend, even if the words he had used for the last message seemed strange to her. And indecipherable.

Nevertheless, those small attentions put her in a good mood and, without actively seeking them, she would have continued to take what David would have given to her.

Absorbed in those considerations, she did not notice Nina's arrival.

"Hello darling! Sorry if I've only arrived now, but the post-Christmas period inexplicably increases traffic…"

"Hello Nina! Don't worry, in fact I thank you

for allowing me to be like a real Milanese here at the Duomo. I was just enjoying my coffee. How are you?"

"Very well, holidays spent wonderfully with my sons. Christmas has become a rare opportunity to see them and yesterday I played none other than the *Befana* for my grandchildren. What about you?"

"I too have been with my family, my father, my friends... I came back a few days ago. It was nice, even if with my dad... well, we can't really have an idyllic relationship, because of all the issues that have occurred. We often argue..."

"You will see that it will pass. It's a matter of time... Did you know that I spoke about you with Alessandra Porri Ranza?"

"Really?! Oh my gosh, how is she? It's been a such a long time since I've seen her..."

"She's now president of a non-profit organization dedicated to the environment, and she's always very busy. She asked me for your number and I gave it to her. I hope you don't mind..."

"Are you kidding?! Of course not! We lost touch because she and her family had moved to the United States. Although there is social media, in the end we didn't look for each other anymore... gosh, I can't wait to see her again!"

"Ah, I'm relieved. Instinctively it seemed nice to give her the number... then you know... doubts came over me."

"No doubts at all, indeed, thank you. I shared a good part of my childhood with Alessandra."

"Great! Now, back to business. These are the questions for your boss", she handed her a packet with a satisfied air.

"Thank you, Nina! David is super happy to do this interview and you were very kind to grant it."

"You know I'm not that kind of journalist. I've been meaning to do it for a while. Let's say that you have facilitated and accelerated the process. Your company is interesting and very promising. You'll be there too, right? I don't exclude that I may ask you a few questions..."

"Absolutely!"

When Nina left her, Francesca looked around satisfied and decided to write to David to inform him. All in all, this was an important issue.

'Good morning David and happy new year! I hope the holiday is going well. Nina just handed me the questions for your interview. When you return to the office on Monday, you will find the document on the table. See you soon, F.'

She didn't have time to put the phone away that David replied.

'Hello... F... I'm in the office. Or rather, I'm in the gym, I'm training. I'll wait for you here, D.'

"Oh!" Francesca exclaimed in surprise and

replied by emphasizing the use of initials. She gloated satisfied, pressing the forward key with enthusiasm: 'Okay, D. I'm on my way. F.'

When she arrived, she immediately walked over to David and saw him punching one of the bags over and over again. Violently.

A couple of colleagues were on the treadmill.

"David!" she said entering the boxing room, "I expected you to come back around the tenth, not right after the Epiphany."

He kept banging and muttered, "I came back earlier."

Francesca approached, slowing down: "Oh, why? Is everything okay?"

"Yeah, everything is okay... So, news with Nina?" David asked between strokes.

"Um... Nina told me that she doesn't know... yet if she will maintain...", she spoke in fits and starts, not sure why David wouldn't stop punching the darn punchball, "the scheme of the classic interview, therefore by publishing the questions and the answers or if she will directly write an article drawing on your chat..."

"The questions? Which ones are they?" He hit the punchball harder and Francesca had to move for fear of being hit.

"Okay, I've had enough!" she finally said.

"Franci, what's wrong?"

"No, actually, David, what's wrong with you?" She glanced at the two other persons in the gym, but they were in the other room, engrossed in their running and isolated in their music.

"Nothing," he looked at her with his usual lively gaze.

"Okay," she said, staring at him worriedly and taking her bag back, "let's do it this way. Finish your training. Later, tomorrow or whenever you want, you will read the questions on your own. I'll be seeing you, Italian Stallion..."

David chuckled.

"Listen, Francesca, I was thinking..." he said, chasing her and stopping her. He put the gloves on her stomach and kept his eyes down, "Today is Friday, many people are still on holiday, there's little work... and... how about a brunch? A picnic maybe?"

Francesca bowed her head and stroked his temple: "Oh my God, it's not that you have a fever is it? That would explain a lot…"

"Ah, ah, ah… no, I'm serious."

"David, maybe you didn't realize it, because the trip to Mauritius has left you hot, but here, in Italy, it's January. January," she repeated. "It's cold. You can't spread out the red and white checkered tablecloth and doze off after you've eaten a couple of sandwiches or whatever, you understand?"

"Why not? I like the idea of relaxing…"

"Someone would find us a little frozen after a while... and I have no intention of indulging this vaguely suicidal whim of yours."

David smiled. "Weren't you the one who wanted to tour the factories?"

"Oh my, you really are sick. What does this have to do with the picnic?"

"Is that a yes?"

"You are crazy!"

David looked at her with his mouth folded in a sly grimace, so Francesca gave up: "All right. And which factory would you like me to visit again? Cesano Boscone's? Or Turin?"

"The one I bought in Ravenna. I'll take a shower and we can leave."

"Hey, what..." she protested, but David had already vanished towards the locker room.

For the entire first hour, the ride was silent. The radio very low, the two of them silent. Sometimes David would turn towards her and smile and she would smile back. At one point, however, Francesca moved forward to see his face and asked him: "Why did you interrupt your vacation?"

The Ferrari slowed slightly and David huffed. "Katrina and I argued..."

Francesca sighed. "So you spent New Year's Eve alone?"

"Not exactly."

They fell silent again until they reached the factory. David got out of the car, opened the gate and on his way back in, raised his eyebrows. "Curious?"

"Quite. Although I don't understand why you had to come here to buy a new factory, far from Milan. And even Turin, it's a choice that I don't understand."

He parked, opened the trunk and answered her. "I'm trying to cut costs... In Milan it has become impossible and although I continue to sign contracts, the fixed costs are very high and the margins keep shrinking."

"So you will close Cesano Boscone?"

"I don't know yet. The fact is that the companies I compete with have moved everything abroad... I at least keep production in Italy..."

He took a picnic basket and showed it to her. "I asked Gianni to stop by this sandwich shop... they also organize lunches to take away..."

"Poor Gianni... but you weren't kidding, a full-blown picnic..."

"I am a man of my word. And I gave Gianni the day off..."

"Oh my God, David, these holidays have changed you... you've gone from despotic to indulgent... you sure you're not sick?"

David shook his head chuckling and took her hand, inviting her to enter. "Well? What do you think?"

He left her, put down the basket and walked to the center of the shed. The black coat he wore spread out like a cape and when it spun back towards him, he looked like a superhero. Handsome and proud, Francesca thought.

"It's very big," she commented, undoing her cache-col and jacket. Strangely, she felt warm.

"Come..." he urged her and took off his coat placing it on the ground. "Sit here."

"No, what are you doing? You'll get it all dirty!"

"Come on, Novelli, for you this and more", he said taking her hand.

David's face was strangely imperturbable, yet Francesca knew he was making an enormous effort to stay serious. He gave her the impression that he meant to hide an emotion from her, because his eyes appeared more glittering. He continued to observe her sideways, while he took out the sandwiches, the goblets, the wine, the water.

"Well, since you've been very successful", Francesca murmured, taking off her jacket, sitting down and glancing at the surroundings, "I imagine your choices are always right... even if it's a matter of dirtying a nice and soft cashmere coat like this, if it serves to admire your new purchase..."

"It's been hard at times and I was often wrong,

but of one thing you can be sure, if necessary, I defend my company with my teeth."

"So tell me, when did you realize that you had finally made it?"

"May I?" he asked, taking the jacket and placing it like a pillow behind his head. He crossed his arms behind his neck, closed his eyes and sighed.

"It was a December day a few years ago. I received an email. I had signed with Peter Hogen... he was already quite successful and for us he would have represented the leap in the big leagues. It was done."

"Must have been a great satisfaction..."

"Eh, but that wasn't what made me realize I'd finally reached success. It was when, a few days later, I crossed the threshold of the Ferrari dealership. You know, it wasn't so much owning the car as it was the ability to choose it. A whim if you like, but one that gave me the measure of success."

"I'm happy for you."

"And, what about you, your memorable moment?"

Francesca stared at him, her mouth curling in a pleased grimace.

"If you really want to know, it was when, that Sunday, you appeared before me and you...saved me," she threw herself beside him and stared at the ceiling. "I owe you a lot, David... I would have ended up in a worse abyss than the one I was already in…"

"Don't exaggerate… you would have bought another phone…"

"I'm serious. And I'm not referring to the cell phone. And you know it."

"Me too, I'm serious. You are a tough woman. Surely it's not me you need."

"But you were there…"

"You are strong, because you don't need anything."

"Why do you say that?" she turned and stared at him, "what is it that's missing in your life?"

"I miss feeling at home."

"Uh, and that's why we're here today?"

David smiled. "That's why you're here today."

His gaze became intense and he pronounced the following words with a transport that was unusual, but sincere: "Franci, I..." he took a breath. "Listening to your voice makes me feel at home, watching you move, makes me feel at home, your perfume makes me feel at home. I'd say three-fifths of me are already home, but…"

At those words, Francesca reacted holding her breath. No one had ever said sweeter words to her. She came closer, staring at him and intertwined the fingers of David's hand with hers.

"To be exact, now, since you're touching me, we're at four fifths…"

She hesitantly asked him, "and what do you need to feel all the way home?"

"I need to taste you…" he answered and stood up, clenching his fingers tighter and leaning over her in awe.

She smiled, answering sensually: "Well then what are you waiting for, come home, David..."

He kissed her slowly, sipping the pleasure, relentless and sweet at the same time, moving over her, but without forcing, just to envelop her, just to contain her in a tender embrace.

It was a long, passionate kiss in which the two, eyes closed, abandoned each other satisfied and finally found each other again.

"David..." Francesca said to him at one point, caressing him, "I don't want to spoil the moment but you have a girlfriend..."

"We broke up. That's why I anticipated my return...", he answered curtly and took her neck, squeezing her to himself. "I kept thinking about you, Franci. I just wanted to be with you."

"Oh... I don't know what to say.. I'm sorry about..." Francesca replied, sincerely mortified.

"I'm not."

The gray space of the shed warmed up and colored with their whispered words, interspersed with sweet kisses on the face and soft caresses. Neither of them was willing to spoil that intense moment, looking deeper; it was enough to look at each other, taste each other, feel each other. Both finally at home.

CHAPTER 12.

The hope of having hit the mark in Francesca's heart this time turned into certainty. However, he was determined to earn her trust, her respect, before taking the next step, the most important one and that would mark a point of no return for him. She was the most coveted destination and he didn't want to risk anything; that's why he had decided to move in small steps, on his toes, like a seasoned boxer.

The following weeks were a continuation of those hours spent at the Ravenna shed. With an unwritten and not even hinted pact, both sought each other cautiously, like two young fiancees, without forcing their hand.

Every morning, David showed up at her front door and took her to breakfast in an always different bar, in a romantic gesture, inspired by his favorite song. Those breakfasts were his way of making her feel that he really loved her, that he loved being with her. And even that morning didn't start all that differently. They had arranged to meet in front of Biffi, where David parked the car.

She was in front of the entrance, her hair moving in the light late January breeze. Leaning over her cell phone, she was passing the time, scrolling through the images and didn't notice his arrival; David took the opportunity to stay a few minutes to admire her.

What he wouldn't do for her.

And when Francesca raised her head, he had to admit that he would have climbed the Everest just to be with her.

"David!" She reached out and hugged him and the craving for physical contact made him tremble.

"Are you cold?" She asked him worried.

He denied it, but couldn't speak right away and stroked her several times with the hand he had free. The other dangled along Francesca's side, due to the small bag he was carrying.

"I'm just glad to see you", he finally answered, giving her a kiss on the forehead, "Come, let's go in."

"Today you are the one who suffers from the cold!" Her scratchy laugh, like a lioness, revived her senses, which resurfaced vigorously. He opened the glass door with such force that he feared breaking it.

"Good morning Mister Trilli!" said the bartender, visibly worried about the door. "In shape as always! Let's hope the door holds!"

"Ah, yes… sorry", he scratched his head, "Good morning to you too… let's sit down in the tea room, over there. Can you bring us two cappuccinos and a couple of your kipfels?"

"Right away, sir!"

"What are kipfels?" Francesca asked him, sitting down.

"A raspberry puff pastry, typical of this café. You want to have a Milanese breakfast, don't you?"

"As you prefer... even if I never come here. Further on is this colonial-style bar..."

"Then tomorrow we shall go there, my princess."

"Ah, ah, ah ... more like a queen ay my age... or queen mother", she threw her head back and the ringlets fell on her chest, as she laughed.

David reached out and took a lock of hers. "How about Empress..."

She flinched as the bartender arrived and waited before speaking again. "I have to acknowledge that the clientele here is very interesting... look at that girl talking to that Japanese couple..." she pointed to a table further away. "Who knows what they're talking about..."

"Ever been to Japan?" He asked, sipping the cappuccino and not paying any attention to the table that she instead continued to stare at.

"No, never and you?"

"No. We can go there together, what do you say?"

"Oh, yeah, yeah, cool. But you have to take me to Nara. Did you know that, speaking of empresses, Nara was the capital of the Japanese empire precisely at the behest of an empress?"

"Expert in Japanese culture?"

"Oh, no, no. Just curious. I read here and there..."

"Then, my empress, we will also go to Nara for breakfast..."

"And where else are you going to take me for breakfast?"

"In every part of the world..."

"Yes, but for me, just empty croissants... not these elaborate and cloying things that you like!" She laughed and he leaned across the table to kiss her, oblivious to the Japanese and other patrons.

"Stop it... everyone is looking at us..."

"I want everyone to know about us..." He bit her lip and took the bag, placing it in front of her. "Here, a little present for you. Before planning any trip, I want to make sure you don't miss... what you will find inside."

Francesca widened her eyes curiously and opened it, peeking. Inside, an ivory sachet. She loosened the closure and a series of sticks of cocoa butter, from the best brands of cosmetics, peeped out.

"But..." she shifted her head alternately to David and the glittery gold pastel tubes. She pulled one out and exclaimed, "Oh, my! Do you know how much this one costs?!"

"Um, not really," David answered awkwardly, "But the salesgirl assured me they're all good."

"Good?! This is the best of the best!"

David scratched his head, "Ah, good. For a moment you made me think I had it all wrong!"

"Oh, no, no", Francesca got up and went to hug him tightly, "Thank you, thank you, it's beautiful!" She kissed him, slowly. "What a beautiful present, David!"

"Mm... now, Franci, even your Japanese friends know we're together..."

"Ah, ah, ah... let's run away then!"

They walked towards the car, hand in hand, to reach the office and David hugged her. He was soon going to propose to her and he was glad he had hired her, because he could relish the sight of her every second of the day.

Just like that late afternoon.

Except that his attention towards Francesca was not attracted by the desire to look at her, but by the high-pitched voice with which she was animatedly entertaining someone on the phone. He decided to go and see what it was.

When Francesca put the phone down, she stared at him worried: "It's about Dotti."

"Uff... what does he want?"

"He learned that production at the Ravenna plant will start in a month and he is even more agitated."

"I don't have to discuss company choices with him. He'll get over it."

"I'm trying to find a solution," she replied uneasily.

"Mm... don't fret over it, the problem is mine... listen, this evening I have that meeting with Mazzanti, so..." He left the sentence mid-sentence and she lowered her voice, reassuring him: "Yes, yes, I know. I organized it, don't worry", she coughed, continuing in a low voice, so as not to be heard by her colleagues, "Ehm, tomorrow morning... breakfast near me?"

"Of course," he said winking, even though he wanted to freely express his feelings. However, in the presence of the other employees it was impossible for him and on this, they both agreed.

"Then off I go! Bye Isa, bye Giorgio!" Francesca exclaimed aloud and set off resolutely for the lift, "See you tomorrow!" She raised her arm in saying goodbye and didn't turn around, but David noticed her sway and the sweet smile she had given him before the elevator doors closed. He smiled too, but more mischievously, because he decided he wouldn't wait until tomorrow to see her again. At the cost of not sleeping.

In fact, once the meeting was over, he launched the lunge he had been putting off for weeks, but which had suddenly become urgent.

He went to the garage, took the Ferrari and traveled the few kilometers that separated him from her apartment. It was nine o'clock in the evening and, luckily for him, Milan seemed deserted, urging him to run to his beloved.

He parked in Via Ruffini, walked quickly to Francesca's building and rang the intercom, putting himself in favor of the camera. He waited for the answer, anticipating Francesca's reaction.

"David?!" Her startled voice made him very enthusiastic and he answered commandingly: "Let me in, Franci."

The sound of the door being opened was prolonged and he made his way to the second floor, on foot, taking the steps as usual, twos and twos. The door was closed and he got nervous. He rang again and knocked lightly. "Francesca, open up!"

"I'm coming!" he heard shouting from within. A couple of minutes passed, she opened it and David thought he was in front of a dreamlike vision.

"Franci. You're…"

"Hi, David…" she said, kissing him tenderly. She straightened her dressing gown and stammered: "I just had a shower", she tightened the waistband and closed the neckline at breast level. She murmured shily, "Come in…"

As David entered, he sensed the unease. Especially his own, because she wasn't just the woman he was forming a relationship with. It was Francesca. The impetus that had brought him there faltered. He took his time, taking off his coat and started to put it on the sofa, but he stopped.

"What happened? Did a suitcase of clothes just explode in your living room?"

"Ah ah very funny!" Francesca bent down to pick up the fabrics scattered on the sofa and on the coffee table. She pointed to some drawings and said, "Look… Isabella made them. In my opinion, she is very good. She could be your next stylist."

"Uhm", he mumbled absorbed more than anything else to observe Francesca's curves, perfectly highlighted by the black dressing gown.

"I was about to eat", continued Francesca, "I have an excellent lasagna in the oven or..."

"Lasagna is fine."

"Heated it with my own hands… as if it were homemade!" Francesca laughed and showed him the place at the table and, turning her back to him, opened the refrigerator. "I can also offer you," she paused and leaned over, "let's see…"

David noticed her shapely, slightly tanned legs. The movements, the dressing gown, the perfume…every element of Francesca contributed to excite him and he knew he couldn't hide those feelings for long. On the other hand, he had realized that not even Francesca had mentioned in the least that he would have to change to eat and that awareness reassured him.

"Uhm... I have this wine... white..." she continued meanwhile, returning to the table and placing the bottle in front of him, "A friend brought it to me."

"Which friend?" David asked him, changing his tone and placing his hand over Francesca's, which was holding the neck of the bottle. She turned to stare at her intertwined fingers and answered weakly, "You don't know him. A friend... David... let go..."

"Tell me who it is." He scrutinized her and felt her agitation and that made him even more aroused.

"David," Francesca insisted, "I said let go."

"The name."

"Michele De Lissi, but you don't know him." This time she looked at him more resolute and tried to spread her fingers to free herself. He squeezed tighter, exclaiming: "Michele... from Laura?"

"Um... yes, that's him."

"Do you see yourself with this guy?"

Francesca let out a big laugh and threw her head back. "Of course not! He is married! With Laura, to be precise!"

Meanwhile, David had stood up and, with his

other hand, had encircled her waist, but without pressing. "That doesn't necessarily mean he's not open to other relationships."

"David... I'm only seeing you..."

Their faces came closer and she reiterated: "He's just a friend, David, seriously..."

"Where does he live?"

"In Ravenna."

"And this guy... this... married guy", he emphasized, further lowering his voice, "... did he come from Ravenna to Milan, just to bring you a bottle?" His eyes widened in disbelief and he lowered even more on Francesca, who, face up, replied swallowing and struggling to pronounce the words: "Yes, but it happened a few weeks ago... we've known each other for some time..."

"I love your naivety…"

"I'm not naive... I'm friends with... his wife... our fathers work... they worked in the ceramics-"

David dropped the bottle and squeezed it, brushing her lips. "Franci... you're sensual..."

"We haven't opened the wine yet and you're already talking nonsense."

"Very funny…"

The oven's timer rang and he snorted. "Make it stop!"

"Yes, but..." Francesca hesitated, but David pressed her further and as she took small steps, he lifted her dressing gown.

"Oh…Da-vid…what are you…" she stammered.

He took her face and first kissed her delicately, leaning on her lower lip and biting the farthest corner, but then he moved her onto the refrigerator and began to kiss her with an impetus for which she evidently wasn't prepared. His hands, strong, vigorous, in an instant were everywhere and she fought to try to appease that ardor. And the more she struggled the more David kissed her neck, chin, cheek and then vehemently returned to her mouth, while her fingers did the same further down, in a diversified attack. The more she tried to stop him, the more he wanted her.

When he realized she was frowning at him, he chuckled and dragged her into the bedroom, guiding her movements. However, he realized that the submission Francesca showed, the docility with which she was letting go, were fake, because at times, she was the one who dominated him.

It was an even game.

He undid the waistband of his negligee and she unzipped his pants. David stroked her shoulders and pulled off her dressing gown, moaning, and she sat on the bed helping him to take off his pants and underpants. Francesca's fingers delicately caressed his skin making him shiver. He accompanied her gestures by stroking her head in a circular motion. The sight of those curls heightened the desire to possess her, but Francesca stopped. Frowning, she kept her hand steady on his left hip.

On a tattoo.

"David, what is it?"

"A sin of youth…"

"They look like initials. D and F..." Francesca murmured again, following with her index finger the path of the black line that formed those letters.

"They're just letters," David told him and lifted her by force. He began to draw an invisible line on her body starting from the shoulder, and then continuing along the breast, on which he insisted for a long time, with circular movements.

The more she gasped, the more he kept licking, until he headed down to her groin.

To where her scar was. And where she grabbed his wrist and stopped him.

In unison, they lowered their faces to their motionless fingers, inches from the scar.

"Don't-" Francesca said.

"Shh…" he told her and continued undaunted, kneeling at her feet. He kissed her spot and mumbled, "It's just a scar, Franci. I want you as you are, I want you this way..."

The sudden movement with which he forced her to lie down did not take her by surprise as his words had done. Sweet and peremptory words and therefore she warmly welcomed him in her arms and between her legs, kissing his chest and urging him to join her.

"Push," she whispered and he didn't hesitate, throbbing vigorously, because he knew that was what she wanted too, because they shared the same urgency. The urgency of loving each other.

When David felt unable to continue, he took her face and kissed her passionately.

"Yes..." Francesca threw her head back, bringing her arms up to underline her surrender and David pushed one last time, literally falling on her curves, which he began to slowly caress. He then slipped his head between her neck and shoulder, inebriating in her scent.

Her deep breaths gave him a whole new sense of belonging.

"David…"

"Yes?"

"I wanted to..."

"I'm not moving an inch from you," he said pressing more.

"Ah, ah, ah", Francesca laughed softly, "you're a real tyrant... no... it's just that I... wanted to know the meaning of those letters..."

"Uhm," he mumbled his lips on her neck, "…that was a stupid thing I did… I wanted to…"

Francesca tried to turn around to look him in the eyes, but he pressed even more against the nape of her neck.

"You wanted to impress a girl?"

"Er…"

"David… look at me please…"

He didn't move, but snorted: "I told you… I acted on impulse. I wanted to make… well, yes… a pact with… myself… it happened when Ditali & Filati became mine…"

"Oh God… seriously?!"

"Shh… tomorrow… we'll talk about it tomorrow… in any case, I can't erase it…"

She giggled, he kissed her, nibbling on her earlobe, and finally closed his eyes, falling into a deep, restorative sleep, the likes of which he hadn't experienced in a long time.

CHAPTER 13.

"Has Mister Trilli seen my drawings?!"

"Yes, a few days ago. Why do you call him Mister Trilli all of a sudden?" Francesca laughed, putting the needle back.

"Because the thought that the boss has rated my creations makes me shiver!"

"Don't worry, he liked them. A lot," she exaggerated a little, but it felt right. "Are you done?"

"Yes."

"So, let's put it on the mannequin. I have to see if the shoulders fall well or if there is still something to do."

They adjusted the dress on the bust and concentrated on the back.

Francesca held a few pins between her lips and, while she pinned a couple, she muttered: "Uhm, here we will put the zipper."

She put away the unused pins and added proudly, "I've managed to find one that's perfect! After, I'll show you. Okay, let's spin it. Oh… simply gorgeous!"

Both observed the result of various evenings spent sewing and Francesca said satisfied: "Isa, you have to try it on! Absolutely!"

They moved to the entrance, in front of the mirror and Isabella adjusted her ponytail. She looked back and a gasp of emotion escaped her.

"Oh my, Isabella... it's beautiful! Can you believe it? Your design has come to life! Brava!"

"Francesca," she said trembling, "I never thought I'd see one of my ideas become a reality and with these fabrics... you were phenomenal."

"*We* were phenomenal. Use the plural. And anyway, I'll give you that it was the result of a tireless cutting and sewing work, but I insist in saying that you are the real architect. This reference to the clothes of ancient Roman women allows you to hide the cuts and imperfections of the remnants and-"

Isabella hugged her tightly and Francesca, after the first moment of bewilderment, reciprocated, caressing her. "Isabella, seriously, I'm not just saying it... I really think you're good at this."

"Thank you, thank you," she replied unable to hold back her tears, "without you..." She stood up and wiped her cheeks, laughing, "I mean, my boyfriend tells me I'm good, but you know how men are... sometimes I think he says nice things, just to make me happy. Am I right?"

"Ah, yes, I know, I know..."

"But a compliment from you, from a woman, with your experience… it means a lot to me."

"Thank you for how delicately you touched the age button..." Francesca answered, laughing.

"No, no, I really mean that you are an expert in the field."

"Now don't overdo it. Expert is a big word."

"It's true! Who would have thought of using leftovers in this way!"

"Well, let's hope it's really feasible on an industrial level. I'm really curious to know what Dotti will tell us next Thursday. Of course it would be nice for our company to start your line. I can already imagine the voice from the loudspeaker during a fashion show: ladies and gentlemen, the designer Isabella Bucci, for Ditali & Filati! It sounds good doesn't it?"

"For me, it sounds magical…"

Francesca's phone lit up. "Ouch, I guess I have to get ready... as I told you I have an appointment."

"Oh, okay, sure."

"Isa, why don't you take the dress home? That way you can show it to your boyfriend and the two of you can fantasize on your sizzling future. I foresee big changes coming your way!"

"Thank you, Francesca, thank you!"

"This is all your doing, dear. I just helped you make your dream come true. Fingers crossed for when we present our proposal to David."

"Yes! Fingers crossed!"

Francesca waited for Isabella to leave before getting off and joining David in a neighboring street, where they had agreed to meet.

David was leaning on the Ferrari, waiting for her. She observed him for a moment: the coat unbuttoned in the front, the confident movements with which he scrolled through the mobile phone, the mischievous expression, the slight beard, which emphasized the manly face. Francesca imagined herself meeting him at the altar and gasped with emotion.

"I'm here!"

"Hello love! Finished the five o'clock tea with your friends? Ah, listen, I couldn't find a parking spot here. I'm sorry", he said kissing her, "let's go to the restaurant. It's near my place so I can park there."

Once they arrived in Via Brera, they walked arm in arm to the restaurant where they were going to have dinner.

February had just started, but the days were mild and the walk on the cobblestone street was pleasant, as they passed the fine arts and antique shops that made that part of Milan so quaint. With each step, as they drew closer to the restaurant's entrance, Francesca's happiness grew. She still couldn't get over that love born by chance and that had overwhelmed her like a river in flood. The feelings she had for David were different, new, probably the most genuine she had ever had for a man. Compared to the previous ones, in fact, the harmony that was emerging was profound, both physically and mentally.

"My, how pensive you look, Franci..."

She squeezed him tightly and pulled herself up to whisper what she thought: "Why, Mister Trilli, I think your love is literally knocking me out, just like the fine boxer you are."

"Not a bad idea, Miss Novelli. I think Sunday morning we'll go to the office to try out the ring… ouch… ouch", he chuckled, while Francesca hit him with gentle punches in the stomach.

"Stop it, I didn't mean that… I meant that-"

He took her hands and brought them over her shoulders, to the back of her neck. "I know, what you mean", he girded her and lifted her, "…you Franci, you drive me crazy…"

"Hey, don't blame me for your craziness. I'm not your wife yet."

"Well this crazy man of yours is hungry," he said.

She smiled and stroked his cheek as they entered the restaurant, continuing that pleasant conversation at the table, based on amorous skirmishes, with David who didn't even leave her hand while they were deciding what to order. David finally settled for *risotto con ossobuco* while Francesca opted for a *polenta* with porcini mushrooms.

"Listen David, I won't be able to be with you tomorrow evening", she informed him trying to hide a hint of bitterness; it had suddenly become impossible to stay away from him.

The sommelier in the meantime had arrived with a bottle of Barolo that David was studying. He nodded in approval.

"Nonsense", David muttered as he swirled the wine in his glass.

"David I'm serious."

"Me too," he smiled, clenching his fingers.

"Let me explain. I invited an old acquaintance of mine to dinner and-"

"Invite her to our house, then."

"In what sense, ours? I know that the apartment is yours…"

Francesca rolled her eyes and pulled to free herself from her grip, but he didn't let go and brought her hand close to his lips, caressing the back as he specified: "I was talking about my house."

"I don't understand…"

"Franci, I think it's time for the two of us to start living together. Seriously though, not like we've done so far, a little here, a little there. I think my house is perfect for two", he sneered and continued, "Besides, I would like to knock you out for good", he rubbed his mouth on her hand, "put some blame on you… and living under the same roof, you will have no more excuses , no?" He chuckled again and stared at her with head down, chin and mouth on her fingers, waiting for her reaction.

"Sorry, wasn't it you who didn't want to mix business and pleasure?"

"Indeed. There, you see? This change in my approach to life is a flaw for which you will have to take full responsibility…"

"Are you serious? Isn't it a little early?"

"Early?! I can't wait and I've never been as serious as I am right now."

She stared at him intently and intertwined her fingers. "Ok… with this… you definitely knocked me down…"

"Is that a yes?"

"Gosh," she swallowed, trying to hold back her emotion and began to nod, wiping the corner of her eye.

"Well?" David was impatient.

"Yes! Yes!" a high-pitched voice came out of her, "Yes! Of course yes!" she laughed and settled back in here chair. "But you are mean to tell me this here…"

"Why?"

"Well, because we are in public and I can't throw myself into your arms! Actually, you know what? Screw it!"

David laughed heartily as she got up from the table and went to hug him tightly and wholeheartedly.

"I can't wait to start living together!"

"Me too, Franci, me too... and we'll continue the hugs later, don't worry..." he straightened his tuft and went back to swirling the wine.

"Oh God, David!" Francesca exclaimed, returning to her seat, "What should I do with Alessandra?! I have to tell her right away! And then maybe she won't feel at ease if it;s the three of us..."

"Is she single? I could invite Carlo and we'll find some excuse…"

"And your friend Carlo, at short notice, can he join us?"

"Worse case, I'll retire to the bedroom and wait for when you finish," he said, raising his eyebrows, "but absolutely, you're having this dinner at my place. At *our* place."

Francesca folded her mouth and stroked his face. "You are so sweet. David I… love you."

He kissed her palm. "Call her, so we can arrange it. I'll take care of Carlo."

"Yes, I'll do it now."

The following evening the two waited for the guests, preparing the aperitif and the dishes to be served together. David put on some Gershwin, turned up the volume and walked over to her, who was arranging the dishes at the table.

"Princess..." he invited her to the center of the room with his index finger, "care for a dance?"

"We have to finish preparing... they will be here in a moment..."

Regardless of the protests, David took her hands and started to dance slowly, his legs adhering to hers, his chest pressed onto hers and his gaze tense to try to get Francesca's consent, who implicitly lent herself to the game, at first pretending to be angry.

They moved sinuously to the notes of 'Summertime', their breaths intertwined, occasionally touching the skin of their cheeks. Francesca let herself be carried away, docile, rubbing his tense muscles, increasing that subtle pleasure deriving from knowing that he was her man. When David took her leg and wrapped it around his side, she leaned back, anticipating the night ahead. The music faded to an end and David lifted her, with a passionate gaze.

"You'll embarrass me if you keep staring at me like that."

"You'll have to get used to it, then... what time did you say they arrive?" His hand slipped under her skirt.

"Don't you dare, Trilli, there's no time..."

"I think so..."

"David, we can't make love every hour of the day!"

"Why not? I love you every second of every hour!"

"Oh, David..." she stroked him warmly and he pushed her against the wall, sharply. "I want you, Franci..." she whispered and didn't lower his eyes as he lifted up her skirt, pulled her underwear aside and took her, kissing her passionately and leaving her breathless. Francesca surrendered to the pleasure. With her ex-husband everything was more routine and not very romantic. Instead, with David, she reached heights she had never reached before and wondered which Olympian gods she should thank for letting him into her life.

The ringing of the bell interrupted the idyll.

"It must be them..."

"Wait..." David told her, reaching the pleasure.

Francesca let out a little cry and whispered: "Oh... my... David... oh..."

The intercom rang again. "David, quick! How do I look?" She smoothed her dress.

"If I were a painter Franci, you'd be my muse..."

"David, come on, I have to go and open the door. Come on, be sincere. Am I presentable?"

"You are the most beautiful woman I have ever seen..."

"Uhm yes... after Katrina and the others..." she commented with a touch of jealousy.

He caressed her cheek and said to her seriously: "Franci, since you reappeared in my life, that September day in Ravenna, I haven't made love to her."

Francesca staggered and frowned as she moved towards the entrance. She pointed at him and slurred nonsense. "You... oh... what... do you mean... I.... do you... mean... I... are you serious?"

The sound of the intercom became insistent.

David laughed: "Very serious. Open up. I'm going to change. Tell them I just got back from the office."

Continuing to look at him, while pressing the intercom, Francesca greeted the guest: "Alessandra, hi! You have to cross the courtyard. We're on the third floor."

She knew her voice was higher than usual and she hoped she sounded calm, while deep inside she felt like a volcano about to erupt. What David had confessed to her was more overwhelming than the foray he'd just given her. His unsolicited fidelity, even before becoming a couple, was a profound declaration of love. It's unusual. She didn't have time to elaborate and promised to clarify with him later. She took a look in the bathroom mirror, finished settling herself and ran to open the door, out of breath.

"Franci!"

"Ale!"

The two women embraced and scrutinized each other to find the girls of the past.

"Please come in and make yourself at home. David will be here in a minute," she blushed and rubbed her skirt several times. "I'm so happy to see you again Ale..."

"Wow, what a beautiful house and you... you, you are always the same, Francesca, what is your secret? I'm guessing this man of yours..."

"Oh, well, yes, I admit it", she smirked, thinking back to what had happened earlier and leaned against the wall, as if to hide her prank, "you find me better now. I wasn't so beaming a few years ago."

"I heard about your troubles, about your divorce. I wanted to call you, but I confess, I was overcome by a feeling of cowardice. You know, calling you to ask you how you were doing, knowing that it wasn't a good time, well..."

"No worries. But tell me about you and your life! How are you? I find you very, very well..."

"Oh, well..." she pointed to her ring finger with no ring, "I got separated too, but not as lucky as you. That's why you piqued my curiosity with this dinner with old friends. What's the guy like?"

"Oh... I..."

"Good evening, Alessandra!" David arrived smiling, saving her from that curiosity she couldn't satisfy.

"David Trilli. Pleasure."

"My pleasure, David. I'm Alessandra Porri Ranza", replied the friend, throwing a sidelong glance at Francesca.

The intercom announced Carlo's arrival and David walked away, allowing Alessandra to comment, quietly: "I mean, I mean Francesca, how cool is he?! Quite the opposite of that awkward ex-husband of yours. Guess you found the right one! Trust me... and let's hope the friend is vaguely of the same species..."

"Ale! I remembered you as more chaste!"

"Sure, me too, but you know how it is... with age you reach a certain degree of wisdom."

They laughed and David turned as he answered the intercom: "Come up, you old fox!"

Carlo was a man of David's age or so, more robust, but pleasant and once the introductions had been made, the four sat down at the table to chat.

"Carlo and I met at a kick boxing class. We beat each other up!"

"Eh, yes, and what drinks afterwards!"

"Yes! And our coach insulted us, because we didn't follow a strict diet as he would have liked..."

"Did he insult you?" Alessandra laughed and

Carlo replied: "Yes! But who was listening to him! He was possessed... do you remember what he said?"

David tried to remember. "He said. Wait... well, yes... the principle of martial art is not the art, but what is hidden deep inside you... or something like that... ah, ah, ah", the laugh that escaped him infected the others, "the two of us were obviously alluding to something else... sorry, sorry... let's change the subject..."

Carlo wiped his eyes. "You're right David, enough about us. You two, Alessandra, how did you meet?"

"It's all our grandmothers' fault!" the woman answered trying to be nice, "At the time, I lived in Milan, but in the summer I went back to Lugo-"

"Oh, where I was born," David exclaimed smugly. He looked at Francesca with sweet eyes and murmured: "Could it be that we also met at the time?"

"Maybe..." she replied and gave him an inquisitive look. She wished she could be alone with him and clarify what he had confided to her before dinner.

"And what do you do now, Alessandra?" asked Carlo, glossing over the two lovers and concentrating on the woman.

"I run a non-profit organization that has become over time an important voice in the world of eco-sustainability. In particular, we take care of making companies aware of limiting waste, waste, of any kind."

"Interesting," Carlo stated with some emphasis, "The company I work for deals with waste storage and I would like to be able to contribute in some way. We too are at the forefront of these issues."

"Really? That would be great! The Foundation always looks for companies that can concretely represent the various issues addressed."

"Well," Francesca indicated the plates, "while you talk about the environment and waste, let me take these away, to make room for dessert."

David followed, carrying some crockery and cheerfully saying, "Here's more waste."

"Did you tease me earlier?" Francesca's voice was serious.

"Okay, I'll deal with the trash…" he replied, opening the trash.

"No I meant, when you told me that you…" she blushed, "that you haven't done that with…her…since you and I got together…well, you told me this, shall we say, cuteness, just to make me happy ?"

David took her waist and kissed her neck. "You know I'm not the type to talk nonsense... it's the truth, however, if you don't believe it, I can't force you."

"I believe you, I believe you", she looked at

him indulgently, "... let's bring the tiramisu to those two, even if it seems to me that they don't miss us at all..."

The evening went on pleasantly and they talked alternately of travel, holidays and each other's hobbies, until they decided it was getting late.

"Are you with a car?" Carlo asked the question coughing awkwardly and Alessandra replied by fluttering her eyelids: "Ehm, no... I came on foot. I live nearby."

"I can drop you off if you like."

"That would be nice of you, thank you."

The two went out and Francesca, closing the door, commented laughing: "I think love has struck here..."

"I don't know... your friend is too passionate," David chuckled.

"And your friend evidently likes pasionarias..."

"I'll gladly leave them to him... I prefer a different type of woman", he patted her side. "Even if you are distrustful..."

"I'm not wary, it's just that..." she decided to be blunt, "Katrina is beautiful and you..."

"Uff... I don't want to talk about her... she may be beautiful, but she's not for me, how can I convince you of that?"

"Okay, you convinced me", she reassured him

and trying to change the subject, she took advantage of the argument brought up by Alessandra to explain her idea to him. "Listen, about what was said tonight about waste…"

"Yes?"

"We too have those scraps of fabric stock that are a pity to throw away. They are very beautiful and with those pieces I got in Cesano Boscone, for example, I sewed that cache-col that I'm proud of and..."

"Yes, beautiful, but I like your neck without scarves. By the way, let me check…"

"David, let me go," she said half jokingly, but he pushed her into the room.

"Do you see that I'm right to doubt your abstinence? You are a glutton!"

"Only of you though! And before, unfortunately, I did a much too quick inspection…"

David turned off the light and the darkness lit up with their laughter.

When the alarm clock projected the time on the ceiling, a few seconds before the sound, Francesca stretched her arm on the bedside table, to turn it off in time.

"David, wake up," she whispered softly.

"Today, let's skip"

"Ah… no… Giorgio wrote to me yesterday evening at nine for this morning's risk committee. He says it's urgent and important, so your presence is needed."

"Ugh, fine, but tomorrow we take a day off. I need to be with you," he kissed her and she pulled away, saying, "You're clingy! Come on boss", she grabbed his hands and pulled him, lifting him off the bed.

"Uff... at your command, princess."

The colleagues were already gathered when they arrived, and Giorgio, serious as always, greeted them only with a nod.

David sat down trying to defuse. "What sad faces, have you all had your espressos? Shall we call the bar?"

"David. Last night at eight-thirty we were served this writ by an employee," Giorgio slid the writ onto the table.

"Okay, it's not the first time... by whom?" he asked leafing through the pages of the document.

"From Paolo Dotti. The problem is that not only did he get us the deed served, but his lawyer also informed us that they have collected the signatures of the other employees and that, if we don't agree with him, there will be some kind of massive lawsuit."

Francesca observed David, who, standing, was bending over the act, absorbing Giorgio's words.

Never would have she expected the violent reaction that followed.

"So," David began, his voice getting louder and louder, "Dotti collected the signatures and we don't have the slightest cover?! In terms of human resources, we didn't know anything about this?"

The colleagues turned to Francesca, who swallowed.

"Indeed," Micaela began, "we had gotten wind of it."

"And you didn't do anything?!" David asked incredulously.

"No. And she", Giorgio pointed to Francesca, "said she would solve it… by talking to them!"

"Is that so Francesca?" David's voice was suddenly dark and his amber eyes streaked with black.

"Yes, that's right, I'm trying to find a solution and I've agreed to meet next Thursday. I think there is some leeway, but I wanted to tell you about it-"

"Some leeway…" David repeated her words cutting her off. Francesca caught the irony of the inflection and therefore tried to explain better what she meant.

"David, Paolo Dotti is perhaps the most senior person in your company, indeed he will retire in a year and-"

He interrupted her again.

"And after a lifetime spent in this company, he wants to change *my* rules?"

"Sometimes a change can be good, don't you think? You know he's afraid you'll close the Cesano Boscone warehouse. We just have to guarantee him that—"

"What are you saying, Francesca! I can't guarantee anything to anyone, least of all to someone who will no longer be with us in a year! How do you think I can guarantee each of my employees that things don't change?! Do you really think it's easy to run a company?!"

"No… but if you can find a way to-"

"Dotti is suing me and you think he will accept an agreement? In my house, this is called extortion. Blackmail! Shit!"

"You hired me because I'm good with people… and I'd like to share an issue with him and… I would have told you about it, but… I'm surprised too… I didn't know he was going to serve the lawsuit. Let me talk to him, I'm sure he'll withdraw everything. Let me explain you my idea… I think it could work. You yourself initially improved production, even increasing work. You told me that, remember?"

"Let's hear it, Novelli," he said sarcastically and raised his voice, "since when do you want to teach me the trade?! You who have never had to work and who have this job, thanks to me?! Why do you think I hired you, if not because you were in trouble?!"

Francesca suffered those words as if they were the punches that David threw on the punching bags. She swung left and right, before standing up and saying softly, "I don't need your charity, David…"

"Francesca look, I'm sorry... I didn't mean..." he began to say, trying to take her by the arm. The stony gaze with which she froze him made him give up on the intent, although he followed her towards the exit, pleading with her. "Wait don't go, let's talk about it..."

She opened the door to the meeting room, nodded to her colleagues and stared at him disappointed: "Go back to your employees, David. They really can't teach you anything. After all, isn't that how you like to lead your life? Alone?"

"No, Franci. I was wrong, seriously. It's just that I'm upset… and…", he tried to stop her, but she broke free, took her bag and headed for the elevator.

"What do you want me to tell you, David? You were nice to hire me, but I don't want you to expect me to return the favor," she choked back tears, even though the words came out broken.

"Tell me, did you take me to bed just because your model left you? Because I was an easy prey at the time? Just to fill the void waiting for the next woman, telling me all that crap about your withdrawal, caused by just seeing me again?"

"No, no, no… Franci… what are you saying? Let's talk about it. Let me explain."

The elevator opened and David tried to get in, but she stopped him.

"There's nothing to explain... I helped you get the interview with Esti and, afterwards, to have fun. How stupid of me to not understand immediately your intentions. But then again, you were right. I am naive after all."

"No, Franci, no… you're wrong. Please listen to me!"

"I'm tired of being around men who make fun of me, who measure my soul with money… I thought you were different."

"But I am different! And those words came out wrong. You have to understand me, when it comes to the company, I get hyped up and talk nonsense! Please forgive me!"

Francesca pressed the button on the ground floor and looked at him one last time. "I'm not one of your Katrinas and I don't need your money, but know one thing, David: my feelings were sincere…"

"I too am sincere!"

"Yes, I agree. I have just had a dose of your sincerity in the meeting room."

The doors closed and David pounded on the elevator that was taking away the one true love of his life.

"Franci! Francesca!" He kept yelling her name and turned towards the meeting room, where Isabella had come from.

"Call Dotti! I want him here, now!" He pounded the elevator again, yelling, "Franci! Don't go!"

He picked up his cell phone and dialed her number. In vain.

CHAPTER 14.

Later, due to a strange twist of fate, it was thanks to David that Francesca managed to find a way out of the impasse that had arisen after she had left Ditali & Filati. In fact, on the strength of that experience, she proposed herself as public relations manager at Alessandra's Foundation.

One of the hot topics, followed by the non-profit organization, concerned textile waste and Francesca was assigned to that area. For several months she had been going back and forth from Ravenna to Milan, but she didn't dislike this new life. Only in the evening, in bed, did she miss David. His hugs, his laughter, his amber eyes. And in the dark, she retraced that last day, when she had gone from heaven to hell.

Speaking of hell David's words still burned, like tattoos etched into her skin. Like her scar. He'd been rough and brusque and unforgiving, but deep down she knew it was the truth that had hurt her. For this, she had fought, recovering her dignity with an economic autonomy finally free from sentimental ties. Her heart, on the contrary, gasped desperately, entangled in the spasmodic search for David among the memories of that love that was fading.

The phone vibrated and she sighed to chase away the lump. She simulated a cheerful inflection: "Good morning, Ale!"

"Hello Franci. How is it going?"

"Fine thanks. You?"

"Good!" Alessandra took a deep breath and, changing her tone, confessed: "The other evening, with Carlo, we went to dinner at David's place."

"Ale", Francesca went back to being gloomy.

"I want to be honest with you, Franci."

"Okay. You told me. And I don't want to hear anything else."

"Okay... it's just that... I feel guilty. You and him were a good match and he asked about you and… look he's obviously still in love-"

"Ale. Please. Please, I don't want to get angry. I am not in the mood."

The friend hurried to change the subject: "Okay, okay... let's talk about work. I called you, because Stefania wasn't sure you would accept the mission."

"Sounds like a movie. I didn't think I would be part of a spy ring!" She laughed.

"Well, it's about attending a conference organized in Accra. In Ghana."

Francesca got up. "Accra?"

"That's right. Lately the community of Kantamanto, in Accra, has been at the center of many debates on sustainability, due to the fact that western textile waste flows there. For this reason, together with two other associations, we have organized a conference there, in a couple of days and you will have to go and represent the Foundation. The various experts will take turns on stage and you will have to participate only as a guest; a discreet presence. I should have gone, but I have a prior engagement and I can't. With Stefania, we have already set everything up. The plane, the hotel. You are the only part still missing."

"Uhm, let me think…" she sneered, "Okay! Of course yes! Accra… wow, it will be my first time in Africa!"

Traveling for work, Francesca knew that being a tourist was really an impossible mission, but she hoped to be able to visit some characteristic places of the African city. Unfortunately, she didn't take into account the timetable of her flight and when she arrived at the hotel, being very late, she immediately went to bed.

The next morning she awoke with a certain appetite. Breakfast was served in a large dining room decorated in a colonial style. Her dark glasses placed a barrier between her and the other patrons she would speak to later, and she was relieved to see that no one she knew was seated at the tables. Before she could have any kind of conversation, she absolutely needed to get some coffee.

"Hello ma'am, the room number?"

"214," she replied in broken English.

"Ah, 214… please sit wherever you like. The buffet is at your disposal. What can I get you?"

"A coffee please."

She wandered around the buffet, pausing here and there and admiring the various local delicacies. Among others, the typical dish of beans and rice, whose name she read, but didn't even try to remember. She sat down again at the table, with her usual simple croissant. That would have been enough, given that a coffee break and a light lunch were planned. She waited for the coffee before starting, because she wanted to sip and nibble together. A habit she didn't intend to give up, not even away from home.

"Madam, here is the coffee and the chocolate pastry, with Ghanaian beans of the Amelonado type."

"Excuse me, there must be a mistake. I only ordered coffee. This," she indicated the pastry, "isn't mine."

"Room 214, correct?" the waiter asked.

"Correct."

"Then it's for you. And this is also for you,"

said the waiter taking something out of the inside pocket of his jacket and placing it on the table, next to the cup.

It was an envelope.

The writing 'For Franci' in plain sight, unequivocally reported David's handwriting.

Francesca turned to the nearby table and glanced at the people sitting around, then looked for the waiter, but he had already disappeared.

"Darnit…"

The discontent was mainly due to the awareness that, she was too curious not to read it. And indeed, she read it.

She opened the envelope and a slip of tissue paper slid across the table. She stopped it with her fingers, while with the other hand she unfolded the letter.

'Franci, I miss having breakfast with you. I miss everything about you. And yet, even if you're not here, you have given me so much. And I wanted to thank you for continuing to be, albeit impossibly far away, my inspiring muse. These months without having you by my side have been terrible, hell, and I still regret having lost you twice in my life. The first, when I was too young and the fear of having you dominated me and the second, because I had the presumption that you were already mine. I had the world in my hands and I threw it away. I was a fool and I'm unforgivable.

That's all.

David.

PS: I didn't do the tattoo on my body for Ditali & Filati; it's a lie that I told you because I didn't feel like telling you the truth. The truth is, I did it for a girl. I did it when, at sixteen, I learned that you had had surgery. If you had a scar, then I wanted to be scarred there too. The original drawing was that of the piece of paper that you find together with these few words. Don't laugh. I was young and as an artist I've always been a duffer, but the intent was to have our initials at each end of a heart. In short, you're right: I'm a cloying man. Filippo, who accompanied me, and the tattoo artist also advised me not to write the names in full. In case things didn't work out, I could have easily fixed the tattoo. I let myself be convinced, but a couple of weeks ago, I completed it, because, for me, you were, are and will always be the only woman in my life.'

The chair creaked. Francesca looked at the drawing David had done when he was sixteen.

She had thrown herself back on the seat with force. She checked again and David wasn't in that room, even though his voice was booming in her head. She even felt his laughter. And what he felt most was missing him.

She lifted her face to fight back the tears and exhaled hard, putting on her sunglasses and taking the letter, the drawing and the envelope, and walked over to the waiter.

"Excuse me, the gentleman who gave you this", she waved the papers in her hand, "has he left yet?"

"Ah, I'm sorry, but I have received instructions from the concierge…"

She didn't let him finish and hurried towards the entrance, nodding to an employee. "Excuse me. I'm Francesca Novelli. I'm looking for Mister Trilli, David Trilli. I would like to know his room number."

"Just a second, let me call the manager."

Francesca's agitation was skyrocketing and she tried to calm down as soon as the manager appeared, but her words faltered as she used a language that wasn't hers.

"As I told your… colleague, I'm looking for… Mister Trilli. He had this letter sent to me."

"Yes, ma'am, but Mister Trilli is not our guest. We have only received instructions to deliver the letter to you."

"Ah, I see," she said sadly and put her arms on the counter as she tried to think. She picked up her cell phone. It was almost nine and the conference would start in less than half an hour and therefore she could not call him. It would have to wait. She wondered how it was possible for David to know that she, of all places in the world, was in Accra that day.

"Alessandra…"

By now it was too late to lecture her friend and she entered the hall where the debate was to be held. She had read the names of the participants, but to be sure she re-read the list on the billboard, which stood out at the entrance. Ditali & Filati was not among them, so she relaxed, put the letter in her bag and taking off her sunglasses, smiled a big smile at the representative of Ghana.

"Mr. Antwi, nice to meet you, I'm Francesca Novelli from the Foundation!"

Her English was rusty, but it only took a few exchanges to recover it almost flawlessly.

"Will you talk too?"

"Oh, no, no. Better leave the stage to the experts, like Mr. Fischer. The Foundation is already pleased to be present as one of the major sponsors of this conference and the projects that will follow from it."

The room began to fill up and the moderator invited everyone to sit down. The German sustainability expert was introduced first and the man dwelt at length on the environmental impacts and in particular on the situation of Kantamanto.

He finished by admonishing the audience. "It is not enough to make a few donations, it is not enough to try to adjust working standards, it is not enough to try to avoid the exploitation of minors. We need to do more! The hope is that together we will be able to organize concrete actions. Thank you."

The applause gave the moderator time to take the microphone again and introduce the next participant.

"We are very honored to have here the newly appointed president of the chamber of fashion as well as managing director of a fabric company that is making its stock remnants its new business. David Trilli of Effe S.p.A."

The moderator smilingly turned towards

David who joined him in great strides, microphone already in hand.

Francesca shivered. She hadn't seen him for months. And his voice reached her in a warm way. Softly. In spite of his terrible English, his affable and smiling manner worked the usual charm. Fascinating. And the monologue was equally compelling. At least for her.

"The production of fabrics naturally determines waste, but we had an idea and we started a clothing production line using just these remnants and as if by magic", he took off his ascot from his neck, "a rag, for example, turns into a scarf. All this by reducing to the lowest common denominator the overall waste deriving from our main activity which is that of producing fabrics, which remains the core business for Effe. A minor line, this one, relating to the creation of garments with waste material, but which has a great environmental impact. And which I hope will be an example for other companies."

The amber eyes pointed to Francesca's, who changed her expression. David continued, "This change in our company policies is the result of a collaboration of various employees. I would like to thank Mister Dotti, who programmed and adapted the machinery of one of our factories", he turned around and applauded Paolo, who stood up awkwardly, "and our very own in-house stylist, Isabella Bucci, who with her creativity has managed to give remnants a new life, transforming them into special and beautiful dresses", he took a few steps back, held out his hand and brought the girl to the center of the stage, who did her utmost to thank him with a few bows.

Francesca clapped her hands harder and Isabella smiled at her evidently satisfied.

"Above all," continued David, "Paolo, Isabella and I want to take this opportunity to thank a person who no longer works with us, but who is here today. If it weren't for her, we wouldn't have embarked on this transformation. Even the new name we have chosen for the company is a tribute to her. Ditali & Filati has grown and has become Effe S.p.A... in honor of... Francesca Novelli. Francesca, on behalf of the entire company, thank you!" He applauded and approached the edge of the stage pointing at her and inviting her to get up. Therefore, in spite of herself, Francesca had to greet the entire audience, who were cheering her on with enthusiasm.

Once the applause ended, David gave her a nod and quickly walked away from the stage, leaving his colleagues to take his place. Francesca expected to see him again in the audience in the row of vacant seats dedicated to lecturers, but he didn't come back.

She felt trapped in the chair. She wanted to get up and go outside to clear her head, but her role prevented it. Furthermore, the fear of meeting David, mixed with the hope of crossing him, stirred a mixture of confused feelings in her, which she was struggling to contain.

When the moderator finally announced the break, she carefully avoided the buffet and headed for the bar, on the lower floor, disappearing before being stopped by Paolo and Isabella.

She tried calling Alessandra, but the number was busy. She sat down on the stool, put down her cell phone and put her hands to her forehead.

"Damn it," she cursed softly. She wasn't sure of anything anymore, because her feelings for David had never really subsided.

"Excuse me ma'am? this is for you."

"Sorry, what?" She lifted her face and the bartender served her a drink, adding: "From the gentleman, over there."

Francesca looked bewildered. David was staring at her, melancholic and motionless.

A ray of sunlight illuminated his face, making him irresistible.

"Excuse me, what is it?" Francesca asked feebly, pointing to the glass and when the bartender answered 'Pesquito', she let go a smile.

"Do you have a pen, please?"

"Sure, here it is."

"Do me a favor," she said writing something on a napkin, "can you deliver it to the gentleman, please?"

Her gaze followed the bartender who dutifully carried the message to David, who changed his expression as he read. He stared at her and then, after hesitating for a moment, stood up with the evident intention of approaching her.

Francesca's stomach twisted, but, deep down, it was what she wanted.

David, hands obediently raised and his tone deliberately low, cautious, indicated the stool next to hers: "May I?" In spite of his cautious manners, he didn't wait for her confirmation, sat down and ordered from the bartender. "Two San Franciscos, please."

"Oh, no, no." Francesca gestured decisively to the man behind the counter and muttered to David, "You're the one who needs booze, not me."

"Indeed, you don't need anything. I find you very well, Francesca. And the San Francisco is not alcoholic," he replied and confirmed the order to the bartender, nodding his head slightly. "At the very least, afterwards, I'll throw myself on your pesquito, even if it's a bit early..."

"Tell me, David, for the pesquito and for the letter, do I sense a helping hand from Alessandra?"

"Not really, that is, in one way it was random. Silvia, your director-"

"Stefania?"

"Silvia, Stefania, whatever. In short, she called

Isabella and asked her if we wanted to intervene as an example of a company that pursues sustainability. Perhaps, this is more of your hand I think…"

"No... I didn't know anything about it..."

"Ah", he exclaimed disappointed and continued, "You know, the trade magazines have highlighted the thing, even after my interview with Esti. I guess that's why. In any case, as soon as I found out, I warned Alessandra, I didn't want there to be any conflicts of interest... she told me there was no problem and then... yes, I admit that I asked her if by chance it would have been you, here, on behalf of the Foundation. Neutral zone. A good place for you to get my apologies. But this," he pointed to the peach-colored drink, "wasn't planned, because I didn't think we'd meet face to face… I didn't even think I'd be able to talk to you… I just wanted to give you the letter. In short, I was wrong. I accept the consequences of my actions. The intention is just to let you know that you have helped grow the company. I am very grateful to you."

"Why did you stop calling me?"

"Because you would have gotten tired and since I'm an asshole like your ex, I was afraid for your cell phone…"

"Ah, ah, ah!"

"It's nice to see your smile again, smell your perfume, hear your voice, Franci", David toyed with a napkin, looking down.

"You always arrive within three fifths of me..."

"A disaster..." He coughed, before asking, "Are you seeing anyone?"

The question caught her off guard and so Francesca sat down on one side, body totally in favor of David, before answering.

"No... I'm happily alone, apart from my father who pesters me... and you? You went back to-"

"No!" He interrupted her, frowning. He turned too, brushing her knees slightly and specified: "Unhappily alone." He puffed out his cheeks, funny grimace, barely pressing his legs on hers, who laughed and reacted spontaneously.

"Oh, you poor puppy..."

She immediately became serious, withdrawing from the light touch, but David stared at her slyly. "Do you know, Franci, that I too have been living in Ravenna for a couple of months?"

"Oh...how come?"

"Because of the new factory... it was necessary to be present to follow the start-up. Going back and forth to Milan was becoming... unsustainable," he chuckled. "Basically, I'm all home and work. And gym. I had one built there too."

Francesca didn't miss the fact that he had puffed out his chest, to emphasize his physical shape, and this heightened the nostalgia of his strong embrace in which, until a few months before, she would have basked in bliss.

With a leap, David got off the stool: "Good. It was a good chat. The drinks are on me, I already told the bartender. Goodbye, Franci. It was nice to see you again."

He left resolute, leaving Francesca disturbed by that meeting that took place on the other side of the world.

CHAPTER 15.

"Mister Trilli is a friend of Miss Novelli, but he's not a relative and therefore I told him he can't access the recovery ward... no... I know it's late for visits, but he demands to speak to her and has no intention of leaving," the nurse was on the phone, glaring at David, who waited patiently.

After a few minutes, a door opened and the doctor came out.

"Mister Trilli? Good evening, I'm Dr. Mezzetti. Listen, Mister Novelli is in an induced coma and if you are not a relative, we prefer..."

"I understand doctor, I really do, and you're right, I'm not a relative. However, Mister Novelli's daughter is a very dear friend of mine and, apart from her father, she has no one to lean on. Please let me in. Just to deliver some things for the night," he raised his hand to call attention to the bag he had, "I'll be out in five minutes. But I think Francesca has been here for quite a while and she may need a break."

The doctor sighed and turned to look at the nurse. "Valentina. Register Mr. Trilli, but everyone else will have to follow the rules. Come", he turned back to David and pushed the door that led to the ward open. "See that dispenser? Put on your the covers for you shoes and wash your hands thoroughly in that bathroom. Beyond the glass door, at the end, is the ward. Miss Novelli and her father are in room number three. Good evening."

"Thank you, thank you, doctor!"

David carefully carried out all that the doctor had indicated to him, after which he entered the corridor dedicated to the most seriously ill patients.

He stopped at the door and craned his neck left and right. The only sounds came from the machines to which the patients were attached to and which alternated in an ominous concert.

He opened it slowly and saw Francesca sitting at the side of the bed, her head buried in the covers, probably asleep. He gently brushed the locks away from her cheek and stroked her hair to smooth them. Francesca opened her eyes, slowly rising.

"David?" she mumbled and stood up, agitated. "David! What are you doing here?"

The lost look made her even more vulnerable and, if possible, even more beautiful in his eyes.

"Shh… don't worry. Silvia warned Alessandra and-"

"Silvia? Do you mean Stefania?" Francesca pursed her lips, as if to laugh and David instinctively passed his finger over her, following the ripple. "Silvia, Stefania, Genoveffa..."

"But... Alessandra is in the United States."

"And I am here. I came as soon as I heard."

Without thinking, Francesca plunged her face into David's chest, who immediately clasped his hands behind her back and pressed hard.

"It's okay, Franci, it's okay", he repeated in a low voice and Francesca's sobs became acute. She articulated the words, in an awkward attempt to make herself understood: "Oh David... we... we argued the last time we spoke and I... hung up... I hung up and now if he... if he doesn't make it, I'll..."

"Shhh... shh... calm down, Franci."

"I- I always ruin- everything, I destroyed my life, my ma... marriage, my relationship with you..., with my dad! I'm a fa... a failure!"

"That's not true! Stop it! You're just tired right now, you'll see that everything will work out..." he squeezed her even more. She then rubbed her face on his chest, inhaled his perfume and stared at him with eyes so sweet and magnetic that David bent down, touching her forehead. He mumbled, "Stop fighting yourself, Franci. You are a good daughter. You are here. And your father is not an easy man, but he loves you and you love him. That's the only thing that counts."

He took her neck and pressed her against him,

enveloping her even more, until she calmed down. Only at that point, David asked, caressing her: "Have you eaten something?"

"I can't get away," she babbled again with a regurgitation of tears. "He might need me."

"He needs you yes but in full strength. Let's get you fed. And if you want to argue, we can do it later. Let's go."

Francesca abandoned herself to his will and put her arms around his neck, letting herself be carried beyond the door. She was too tired to resist.

"Here we are." He set her down gently and pointed to the bag, "There are a few things in there. I brought a travel case with the essentials. You know, toothbrush, toothpaste, and..." he smiled, taking a stick, "the inevitable cocoa butter. Your favorite brand, if I remember correctly. There is also a t-shirt, I didn't know the size, I chose an M. Here," he pulled out a smaller bag, "is our dinner. Over there is the dining room. What do you want to do first? Do you want to refresh yourself first?"

She nodded, trembling like a deer: "You... you shouldn't..."

"Come on," David said, taking her hand, "I'll walk you to the bathroom. I'll be outside."

"Would you do this for me?" Tears filled her irises and David pulled her towards the restroom sign at the end of the corridor without answering. He opened the door and took a quick look, then nodded to her, handed her the bag and leaned against the wall, arms folded. "Pretend I'm your bodyguard. Take your time and if you need anything, I'm right here. I will not move."

Francesca's feeble smile was for him a small confirmation that his instincts hadn't been wrong. She needed him. And he just wanted her to be okay. Nothing more.

When she came out of the bathroom, Francesca's face seemed more relaxed and David took the bag, put an affectionate arm around her shoulders and took her to the cafeteria.

The room reserved for relatives of people in intensive care was the classic hospital room, with white tables and chairs, pale green walls and a couple of vending machines for drinks and snacks.

"I'll get the drinks, meanwhile choose a sandwich and start eating. You need to eat."

Despite being at the vending machines, he followed Francesca out of the corner of his eye, who slowly unwrapped the sandwiches, sat down tired and turned towards him, perplexed.

"It wasn't necessary for you to come here, David... I can take care of myself."

He put down the soda cans and sat down next to her, sighing. "I know Franci, you're strong."

"I'm strong..." she repeated. Then she let out

a sob.

David took her hand. "It's okay, let it out"

"No... it's just that... if he dies, I... I haven't told him that I love him and... without him... I'm left alone, do you understand?! I will be without a family!"

David immediately stood up and hugged her from behind. "What are you saying, Franci? You're not alone. There's me, there's Alessandra... I'm sure there are many people who love you. You will see, you will find a... you will find someone and... you will form your own family. And then," he said sitting down again, but keeping his arm wrapped around her shoulders, "Your father is a rock. He's going to make it, you'll see!"

He laid back, releasing her and continued while taking his sandwich: "I'm not sure you know it, but your father has always been an inspiration for me. I guess I have a soft spot for all the Novelli family," he smiled at her.

"I met him because he had a thing for shoes and my father always sent me to make deliveries. I still remember the first time. I arrived by bike, around five and he was out in the garden, smoking a cigar. As soon as he saw me he gave me this big friendly hello", he imitated it, "and greeted me emphatically. In short, he was one of the few adults who treated me with respect. And I was only fourteen. I still didn't know who you were", he caressed her, "but I knew you existed…"

"So", Francesca asked curiously, "did you and I meet shortly after?"

"Yes, a few months later when school started, but that's a story you know. At that point, though, I always wanted to be the one to do the deliveries. You know… to have a chance to see you. But, I confess, I really enjoyed talking to your dad. You had a big, beautiful house, he was the successful entrepreneur of the area. I wanted to be like him."

"Then I guess you always had a passion for business…"

"One of my few obsessions. And your father has done nothing but encourage it. Every time I came back, he invited me to chat. Politics, above all. I understood little of it, but I was a good listener. And at the end, he would always tip me. Generously. And he insisted. I told him that my father wouldn't let me take anything, that the delivery was already included in the price, but there was nothing to do and-"

"And you would have been a fool not to accept it."

David chuckled. "Yes. However, I never spent that money on stupid things. I saved it. I would go home and put them in a box under the bed. You have no idea how much it helped me when I left Ravenna. That money was my lifeline. So I owe a lot to that man," he pointed down the hall.

Francesca seemed absorbed, so David murmured: "I hope I haven't said anything offensive..."

"He loves people who do things, who get busy. With me, he always argued. And maybe," she exhaled, "Maybe, he was right. I've never fought for what really mattered to me," she looked at him and smiled.

David undid the button on his shirt and rolled up his sleeves: "Franci, you're his daughter. If I had been his son, he wouldn't have let me off the hook on anything… but instead like this, he treated me as a man. Do you want coffee?"

"Yes", she answered softly and once David had moved away, she murmured: "I think maybe you don't know, but I, shoemaker's son, was secretly at the window watching you while you were talking to him..."

The dreamy gaze replaced the worried one and David noticed it. "Did you say something?"

"Ah… yes, no sugar, just black, thank you."

"I know, I know, Novelli prefers a dull life. God forbid you sweeten it in any way."

"How funny… David it's half past nine", she looked at her cell phone, "wait, no, what am I saying! It's already a quarter past ten… you have to go home. I guess you have to go to work tomorrow."

"Yes, I'm off to Milan… we have a board meeting. We do it now that it's the end of August, because then we start again with the fashion week…"

A shadow darkened Francesca's face and David thought he had said something mean, so he added: "If you want, I'll stay. At least until the big nurse comes looking for me."

"No, no, are you kidding? And then they told me that they intubated him, but that if he keeps his lifeline stable, they'll start waking him up tomorrow. Maybe said this just to reassure me…"

"You'll probably need me… I can postpone the board meeting."

"David, don't be silly! No really. You've already been kind by feeding me and bringing me all the night stuff… I don't want to abuse you."

He took her hand and kissed her palm. "You know you ask me anything."

Francesca sketched a smile and he bowed his head, "Let's agree that tomorrow, you let me know how he's faring and I'll try to be back in Ravenna by dinner time. I promise."

He took her shoulders and gave her a kiss on the forehead: "I love you, Franci."

"Drive carefully, please. I'll be here. I won't run away, the big nurse will be watching over me."

"Ah, ah,… I'm glad you got your spirit back. Shall I take you back to your room?"

Her languid gaze did not leave him, not even when, at home, he tried to fall asleep. He lay in bed staring at the ceiling, reflecting on many aspects of his life and only fell asleep, exhausted, at three a.m., but after the alarm went off, he felt refreshed. Of course, the previous day he had acted on impulse and was aware of risking getting hurt again, but he was determined to cultivate that faint hope of winning back the woman he loved.

He set out resolutely for Milan. On his Ferrari, Billy Joel was singing 'New York state of mind'. Well, he was in a 'Francesca state of mind'.

At half past six, he resumed his way back, getting on the A1 highway with the music blaring and the intention of stopping only to get something to eat. He sent her a message: 'I'm on my way, even if I'll be a little late. I'm bringing the food, don't go anywhere.'

When he arrived at the hospital, the procedure for accessing the ward seemed to take forever, but as soon as he saw her, the tiredness completely left him.

Francesca was literally slumped in the chair, her face on the bed, one arm dangling, one leg stretched out. He let out a small laughter because of the absurd position she'd fallen asleep in. She was fast asleep and he bent down to look at her better. The dimple near his lip was becoming permanent, but he loved that dimple. It was the same one that appeared every time she looked at him mischievously, the same one that he had seen on her face, on the first day of school and one of the first characteristics of her that he had fallen in love with.

The urge to kiss her sharpened, as did the desire for her to be his again.

Slowly, Francesca began to slide further down and David, worried that she might fall off the chair. He took the other chair, placed it near the window, placed a cushion between the sill and the backrest and picked her up as gently as possible. She turned and, moaning, hugged him, continuing to sleep.

David breathed again, sat up and made sure she lay on him as best as possible. He caressed her hair and had the distinct sensation of having a beautiful fairy in his arms. His mind finally gave him the adequate soundtrack, but he didn't have time to hum it, because, exhausted himself, he fell into a deep sleep. The sound of machinery drowned out the beating of their two hearts.

Once her eyes opened, Francesca stood still for a moment. Bewildered, at first she didn't understand where she was. Her senses recovered in jerks, one after the other, autonomously, and she slowly massaged her arm to make the tingling that bothered her disappear.

A good smell of almonds and wood surrounded her and her body rested on something hard but comfortable at the same time. In front of her, the bed, the father, the machinery. She tilted her face up and saw David's face.

She stood up a little and looked at him in amazement. He was seated, his head bent on a cushion, which he rested in a fortuitous way against the wall, and although he was asleep, even snoring, he kept his right arm firmly wrapped around her back and, with his left hand, he was encircling her thigh.

Francesca thought she was seeing David for the first time. The unkempt beard of a couple of days even made him appear more handsome than usual and even that mole on the cheek just below the eye was irresistible. He wanted to kiss him right there, but she held back while starting to caress his bicep. She realized that she had missed him during those last months. Greatly. Although he had treated her badly and she had left with the intention of never speaking to him again, in reality, she felt good in his arms. She curled up on his chest again, trying to sink and feel closer to his heart, listening to its beat.

"Hey…" David moved slowly stroking her ringlets. The pillow fell to the floor and she reached for it.

"No," his voice was warm. "Stay," he pleaded and touched her neck, running his fingers gently.

"Did you sleep with me all night?"

"You fell asleep in a bizarre position. The alternative would have been to see you fall to the ground, so..."

"So, you are a really good catcher."

"I would always sleep with you over me," he muttered as he adjusted his tuft, his lively gaze fixed on hers.

Francesca sighed. "I guess I have to get ready for another day. Yesterday in the end, they put off waking him up for a couple of days."

"By the way, I need to talk to you", David said, "Yesterday I hired two nurses who will alternate day and night. They are trusted, they assisted my mother. Doctor Mezzetti is already aware of everything."

"David, I can't pay two nurses and I don't want to owe you anything", she tried to free herself from him, but without success. "I just finished paying you the previous debt..." she said bitterly.

"I'm not doing it for you, but for him," he lifted himself up and set her on her feet. "And for what happened in Milan, for the words I said," he added, "I apologize again, Franci, but what can I do, to make you understand that that day I was beside myself, because I was afraid of losing the company for which I spat blood?! That Dotti, he had been tormenting me for months and the lawsuit... well... I was afraid."

"You don't have to do anything, David. And let's face it, I understand that you only hired me to help a friend. I was the one who deluded myself. Ironically, it helped me, working for you. My self-esteem increased…"

"The truth, Franci, is that I hired you, because I wanted to have you near me, because I wanted you to fall in love with me!" He raised his voice and immediately lowered it, "Sorry, sorry, I didn't mean to raise my voice."

Someone knocked on the door: "Mister Trilli, can I come in?"

David hurried to the door.

"Good morning Luciana, come. Let me introduce you to Francesca Novelli. Mr. Novelli won't be awakened until in a few days, so for now there are no particular treatments to deal with."

"Very well," the woman replied and introduced herself to Francesca. "Pleasure to meet you Miss Novelli, you will see that your father will recover quickly."

"Ah, thank you, thank you…" she replied absently, lost in the words David had just said to her.

"Come, Franci", David gently took her by the arm, "I'll take you home now. You rest a bit and I'll come back to pick you up in a couple of hours. From now on you will stay here with your father, but you will have them to help you too."

Unlike his grip, David's words were firm and she could do nothing but nod. She just wanted to have the opportunity to talk about them again, but in the car, strangely, she didn't find the courage and once they arrived in front of her door, she squeezed the bag to herself and didn't move.

"Something wrong? Is it what I told you earlier? Sorry, you know how I am. This time I really want to help you, but here you brought it up and... Franci please... forgive me?"

"Ehm... well... I... no... that is, yes, it's not for that..."

"Oh, no?"

She shook her head. "No...it's just that... I don't want to be alone."

David acted instantly. He turned the car back on. "You're right, how stupid of me. Let's go to my house. That way I can show you where I live!"

David's house in Ravenna was located towards the small hamlet of Classe, along the Fiumi Uniti river.

"Oh, but it's beautiful here..."

"I'm glad you like it. You will like the little house I bought even more."

In fact, unlike the luxurious and modern apartment in Milan, David's farmhouse in Ravenna was cozy and rustic. As he parked, the red of the Ferrari stood out against the bright orange wall of the farmhouse, creating a crackling color effect.

"Beautiful."

"It still needs some renovating. Here", he pointed to the porch, "I want to make a veranda entirely out of wood with a swing and some barrels. What do you think?"

"Very romantic."

"Good," he said as he opened the wooden door. "Come in…"

He turned on the lights, opened the windows and Francesca had a very strong sensation.

She felt she was at home. She turned to David, seeking his gaze and when she found him, smiling, welcoming, intriguing, her stomach twisted at the thought of having let him go, not having argued, not having argued to the end and not having had the courage, afterwards, to make peace. If they had been honest with each other from the beginning, if he had come out right away, things probably would have turned out differently. Or maybe not?

"This way, Franci. Use the bathroom in the bedroom. It's brand new. I use the other one, which still needs finishing... Franci? Is everything okay?"

"Oh, yes, yes. Thanks David. You're very thoughtful," she replied as she entered the bathroom and David followed.

"I'll only take what is necessary to shave. Um… you'll find some of your stuff you left in Milan. I brought them here with me. I wanted to wait for the right opportunity to give it to you and I think it has arrived..." He scratched his head and pointed to one of the two washbasins, where a perfume that Francesca had bought in Milan stood, along with her brush. "I know. I put them there, because... because..." he didn't finish the sentence and clapped his hands. He pointed to a locker. "The towels are in there."

The embrace of the steam-laden shower was like a healing balm, tenderly soothing her senses. When she finished, she wrapped her hair in a towel and looked at herself in the large mirror that took up half the wall. She couldn't help but linger on the canvas of her reflection.

Her scar lingered upon her skin, and however faded it was from the past, it continued to be her gripe. In her eyes, it persisted as a beacon that illuminated her form, an insistent reminder of its presence. Age, she believed, had granted it an insidious strength, a tenacity that refused to wane.

But now another light distracted her. In fact, she glimpsed the reflection of something very colorful coming out of the window and turned to see better, pushing the curtain aside.

She remained speechless.

Behind the farmhouse, was a small well, covered with majolica and finished with a wrought iron arch, over which a rose plant climbed. Swinging gently in the embrace of the wind, a hammock swayed, suspended between two sentinel trees – a pair of strawberry trees, to be precise. The sight was like a canvas painted by an artist's touch, a masterpiece woven from the threads of nature's splendor.

A renewed determination possessed her.

She took the towel off her head and left the bathroom barefoot, crossing the rooms on tiptoe, not looking around, but simply intent on following the sound of the other shower, to reach the bathroom where David, humming as usual, was washing himself.

"David!" She cried out.

Suddenly not a drop of water came out of the shower head, the glass of the shower opened slowly and he peeped out.

"Franci?" he asked, taking a towel hanging nearby. He gave himself a quick wipe and wrapped it around his waist, still coming out half wet. "Everything okay? Are you sick? Low blood sugar maybe? I'll make you breakfast right away-"

"What game are you playing, David?"

"What do you mean? I don't understand…"

"Are you going to tell me the truth, this time or not?! Are you just helping a friend or are you taking advantage of me again?!"

"Franci", David took a step forward, his eyes widening in a stunned grimace, "what are you talking about, because I don't..."

"The well, David! Did you think you could win me back with four painted majolica tiles and a hammock in the wind?"

He spread his arms, blurting out: "Do you want the truth, Franci? What do you want me to tell you, I love you. But let's make one thing clear: I don't want to take advantage of anyone, least of all you, understand?! I'm not that kind of man... the well was already there... and I admit it, I restored it, thinking of you. Tomorrow I'll have it demolished, but you can't expect my feelings to disappear in a flash. Come on, get dressed. I'll take you back to the hospital. Starting tomorrow you won't see me anymore, if that's what you want."

"What I want, David, you don't even know!" she shrieked.

"Of course I don't know!" he answered just as harshly, "And do you know why?! Because you're too scared to let go, too scared to let someone love you, too scared to reveal your weaknesses," he spoke softly again, "But, Franci, I really love your flaws, do you understand? I love that dimple in your mouth, I love the agitation that assails you if you don't find the lip balm, as if it were a matter of life and death, I love your fragility... your insecurities-"

"Oh really?" she interrupted, "You love my flaws?! Let's see if you love this. Do you know why I have this scar, David?!" The words came out hard and bitter as her fingers touched her left side.

He imperatively took off the towel, throwing it aside and answered her, touching himself on the same spot: "Yes, of course. If you read the letter and I think you did, I have explained the reason for this tattoo."

Disconsolate, Francesca looked at David's colored side. In fact, he hadn't written a lie to her: he had had their full names tattooed. She breathed hard and tried to clarify: "I was asking you if you know why I had surgery, what my condition is..."

"I know. I know everything."

Even though she was surprised that he knew about the cause, she continued harshly: "So do you know or not, that I have half the chance of a normal woman of becoming a mother? And that, if you add the fact that I'm turning forty this year, the chances drastically decrease?! I have little hope of starting a family! This is my fault! And it is not enough to build a well, make it pretty with tiles of various colors and hang a hammock next to it, to grant your wishes, David!" She pointed her finger towards an indefinite point.

David shook his head, with a half grin: "And you, Francesca, do you think I'm interested in your chances of becoming a mother? Do you think I love you conditionally? I just told you that I love you for who you are, not for who you might be!"

"You may have been in love with me from the start, but if you want a family, I can't give it to you! Do you understand it or not?!" Francesca's voice sharpened and gradually more agitated, she continued her monologue: "If you haven't noticed, I'm not young and beautiful like Katrina! Yes, she would give you many blond children with blue eyes. Go back to her and stop tormenting me... what could I give you, what? Only complications. I'm getting in the way of your work, your life, your future," she stretched her arms out to her sides. Proud and afraid. A tear slid down her cheek.

"Are you done?" David finally asked.

That question, which David had asked her in his usual firm and peremptory voice, disoriented her.

She considered the answer. "Um, yes, I think that's all."

David moved forward, slow, like his words. "A family is made of two, Franci. And I want it with you. When you're not here, I'm nobody. When you're next to me, the world no longer exists and there's just the two of us. And when you're away, the world oppresses me. I thank fate, the gods, whoever, that you and your ex" he moved closer and looked at her firmly, "and this, I want to emphasize, is the last time you and I will talk about that asshole... that you, you have not had children. We will have other possibilities. When we were in Accra and I saw you again, well... I thought we might adopt a child. And if that doesn't work either, never mind."

Francesca struggled to hold back a sob, but David was inexorable.

"I can't assure you that there won't be difficult times, because life is unpredictable and I can't assure you that it will be easy to stay with me. I have my flaws. Because of which, I can't even guarantee you that we won't fight in the future, in fact I'm sure we will again. But I guarantee you one thing and one thing only. From now on I'll stay by your side", the hands moved vigorously, the fingers accompanied his thoughts, "You're angry, maybe I'm angry, but I'll stay here. With you. And do you know why I'm sure of it? Why, yesterday I resigned from Effe S.p.A."

Incredulous, Francesca murmured: "What did you do?!"

"Well," he scratched his head and made a mischievous grin, "I still retain ownership of the company and will be the chairman, but our arguments made me think things through. The company needs a change. We need new blood. Me too. But I, Francesca, don't need a wishing well to make my dreams come true. For me it's enough to get lost in your eyes and I know that everything I want has already come true."

CHAPTER 16.

"I longed and at times feared this moment! What other document will they want before they consider us suitable?!"

"Geez, Franci, relax, they're just asking us to do the x-ray of the lungs again and within a month, a month and a half, we'll have our little Denis at home."

She pushed David away and angrily said: "We've been going on for a year, David, they have all the information about us, they know everything about us. And now that we're about to leave, they want a quick x-ray?! Birth parents are not asked for all this! They just conceive! And us? Why is it so complicated for us? Why?"

"Are you afraid Franci?" The tone of David's voice was deep and soothing. It helped to calm her.

She nodded. "Yes. Yes, I'm very afraid, David. What if I'm not a good mother after all? What if I wasn't good enough? I do not know how to do it…"

David laughed softly.

"What are you saying, Franci? I mean you, in one year, have learned Ghanaian in order to welcome him in the best way! And then you have me by your side..."

"You're right David. It's just that I..."

"I'm scared too, maybe more than you. I know I'll be wrong and maybe one day Denis will look at me and tell me that I haven't been a good father, that I'm not his, that I don't understand him and he wants to go back to Ghana to meet his real parents. And you know what I'll do? I'll go with him, we'll go with him, because that's what parents do. We will stand by his side. Always. And even if I can't say in Ghanaian or Akan or any other language in the world, I love you, Denis will understand, because I will teach him to read and play baseball and ride a bike. We will look at the stars together and dream. And above all, I will hug him whenever he wants, I will be there when he will need me. So if I have to show someone that I can be a good parent, that I have enough love in my lungs to pump Denis's heart whenever he needs it, then I'm going to do the fucking x-ray, Franci."

"David… you are… I love you, David", she wiped away her tears, "and this speech… my heart is torn… you are so…"

"To fix your heart, honey, I have an established method", he looked at her brightly and took her by the hand.

"Ah, ah, ah… no, no!" She pointed a finger at his chest, "Don't even mention it now, no way! Come

on, we don't have time. The appointment for that..."
she laughed, "damn x-ray is set for four and the
sooner I do it, the sooner I'll feel better!"

"Ah, what you don't do for your children... all
right, let's go, let's go..."

And David and Francesca did the x-ray, flew
to Ghana and stayed in a hotel where Denis would
meet them regularly, to get used to their presence,
slowly.

On the first day, they eagerly awaited him
with three teddy bears, two large and one small, that
Francesca had bought to play with him and simulate
their future family.

"What if we sat down on the floor? This way,
when Denis enters the room, we will be at his level."

"Great idea, Franci. Hey, why doesn't my bear
have something distinctive? That is, you put your
pink cache-col on yours and mine? Nothing? Couldn't
you have handed him a car keychain or, better, a
baseball mitt and a ball?"

"I didn't think about it, I didn't do it on
purpose."

David leaned back and dragged his backpack
close to them. "I thought about it, luckily. Here it is.
Before you can object", he pulled out a few things,
"the ball is made of rubber, so you don't get hurt, and
I took my historic boxing glove and a small one,
especially for Denis. Also," he took a clear bag with a

long string, "this is for your teddy bear."

Francesca picked up the bag that contained a blue stick. "Cocoa butter?"

"Mm… put it around her neck. Your mama bear will need it before going to sleep, otherwise how will she do it?" He smacked his forehead, teasing her.

"How cute..."

"Actually, I thought they are our perfumes. Cocoa butter and leather… you know, memories are also fixed through the sense of smell…"

"Oh, David, you are very, very sweet", she kissed him on the cheek and at that moment Denis appeared accompanied by the guardian.

The three looked at each other for a few minutes in silence. To Francesca it seemed like an eternity, broken by David's intervention, who moved the teddy bear in his hand making it bounce the ball up and down. He undertook to throw the ball with one arm of the bear and to catch it with the other, the one to which he had slipped the glove. Sometimes the ball rolled on the ground, near Denis' feet. On the third time, David offered it to Denis, who stared at him, bowing his head curiously, but finally let go of the hand of the woman who had accompanied him and took the ball. He tossed it towards the cuddly toy David was holding and sat down in front of the little teddy bear. He looked up at his parents, pulled on the little glove and smiled at David.

They started playing. David tossed the ball and Denis hit it back. They continued in that way, but at a certain point, David involved Francesca and the game extended to all three and after a while, they began to whisper. A few words, a few smiles, a few caresses.

"Oh, gosh!" Francesca exclaimed softly, "Can you believe it David? We're playing, he's playing with us..." She was moved.

"Shh, let's keep playing, until the game becomes reality."

Initially, the meetings lasted a few hours, but thanks to the expedient of the three teddy bears, which Denis had immediately made his own, the understanding grew stronger every day, overcoming the language barrier, with Francesca, who translated for David.

A couple of weeks went by and finally, the last few days, Denis stayed with them for the night too.

That evening, something extraordinary happened. After David had finished reading a story and had closed the book, while he had turned to put it back on the bedside table, Denis asked Francesca directly, without the intermediation of the stuffed animal: "Maame, sen ka medo wo?"

Surprised, her eyes widened and tears blurred her vision, because she had immediately guessed what Denis had asked, not quite correctly. She took a deep breath, before answering him, because she wanted him to understand well: "I love you, medo wo, I love you."

Denis turned to David and climbed onto his chest, putting his little hands around his neck: "I, I..." he peeked at his mother, who suggested the words to him again, and finally, he exclaimed, "... I love you, papa..."

David hugged him tightly and kissed his curly head: "Medo wo, medo wo Denis, medo wo… I love you, too, I love you so much. So so much, medo wo pa ara…"

Back in Italy, the months followed one another quickly, because the presence of a new life among them made everything more pressing and soon it was September again, the yellow leaves, the light rains, which sweetly perfumed the air.

One day David thundered solemnly at Francesca: "Mommy! Denis and I have to go buy a school backpack. Wil you come with us?"

"Oh, this morning? Unfortunately I have to meet Alessandra for work. I have an appointment with her soon."

"All right. And don't worry, we're bringing grandpa too. Look, we thought we'd buy the one with wrestler. What do you think?"

"Oh, yes…" she answered uncertainly and

stroked Denis' curls, "I think it's a great choice."

The boy threw his fists in the air and shouted: "It rocks!"

"Okay…" Francesca touched David's shoulder and said hesitantly: "Are you sure it's a good choice? Isn't that a little too violent?"

David laughed and took Denis by the hand. "Ugh, let's run away, baby, otherwise mom will convince us that it's better to buy the backpack with the pink ponies. Let's go get grandpa."

"Okay… have fun!"

Francesca waited for the three to leave and then took the car to go out too. She felt guilty for not revealing anything to David, but she wanted to do those tests first. She wanted to be sure.

"Francesca!" Alessandra joined her quickly, "I've already asked. Second floor."

"Ale, you are a friend. I'm so worried…"

"Are you joking? I won't leave you to deal with a situation like this."

"I wanted to talk to David about it, but-"

"I understand, don't worry."

The doctor looked at the monitor, turned to her and nodded, serious, but only after reading the report, Francesca realized that she should have involved David.

"Oh God, Alessandra... I... I don't know how to do it..."

The two women went out and a light drizzle began. At times, Francesca stopped and made a smile, at times, she tapped her eyelids, trying to hold back the tears, which instead fell as heavy as drops.

"Do you want me to take you home, Francesca? Leave me the car keys and then I'll come with Carlo-"

"No, no, thanks, Ale. It's all so sudden, but I'm ready. I can go home by myself. And it has also stopped raining."

"Alright, see you tomorrow, okay?"

They embraced tightly and Francesca returned to the farmhouse. It was still deserted and the station wagon, which had abruptly replaced the Ferrari, had not yet brought back her three men.

She went to change and passing in front of the bathroom, she couldn't help herself. She rushed in and vomited. The retching didn't leave her immediately and she remained on the ground, her forehead damp and her body trembling. She began to move with difficulty. She wiped the saliva that had wet her chin, got up and washed her face, glancing in the mirror and that's when she saw the reflection of the station wagon, parked next to the hammock. She pushed back the window curtain. "What the hell..."

David called. "Hello, hello, where are you?"

"At the mall. Are you all right?"

"David, why don't you tell me the truth now?!

The car is parked in the back. What is going on?"

"Ah, ah, ah… I can't hide anything from you. We're coming, we're almost home. Give us a few minutes."

Francesca ran down and went to the gate. The river pass right in front of it. She looked around and in the distance, she saw a man walking alongside a horse with a long mane, a red ribbon around its neck, and carrying a child on its back. David held the bridle and Denis chatted amiably with his grandfather, who proceeded quickly in an electric wheelchair, alongside the horse. Her family, Francesca thought, stroking her belly.

David raised his arm and greeted her enthusiastically.

"We're back!" he shouted at her smiling, "Surprise! Happy birthday, a couple days early, honey! Meet Rocky! Your prancing horse!" He laughed with a mischievous wink and Francesca embraced him stroking the horse's muzzle.

"Thank you, love", she whispered in his ear and then turning to the boy: "Denis, do you like being up there?"

"Yes, mommy I like it a lot. Daddy says you'll teach me how to ride!"

"Oh yes! This is a beautiful horse… is it a Friesian?"

"Yes, personally chosen by Denis. We thought

we'd take him home today, since it's Saturday, because you work on Monday... so", David scratched his beard, embarrassed.

"Thank you guys! Thanks Dad!"

She bent down to kiss her father who said to her: "You've always been a good horsewoman, Franceschina..."

"I learned from the best," she replied smiling.

"Mom, get on, get on!" The boy clapped his hands and Francesca mounted her horse behind him. "David, where are we going to keep him?"

"The stables are right here at the end of the road, you know... Il Corbezzolo?"

"Ah, yes, yes... I get it. Well, then we can go on foot too."

"I'll come too," said Francesca's father, "if it doesn't bother you. It will do me good to be outdoors."

"Yes, grandfather, yes! Hurray!" shouted Denis delighted.

That evening, once the grandfather and son were put to bed, David and Francesca lay down in the hammock, embracing each other.

"David?"

"Yes? Do you want to go inside and pamper us better?"

Francesca laughed and nipped at his ear. "Yes, fine... but... first I have to show you something", she fumbled in her pocket, "This morning I went to do some tests, in the hospital-"

"Franci!" David scrambled up and the hammock nearly flipped over, "What's wrong?"

"Relax stallion, don't get mad... everything is okay..."

"Franci, don't joke, I'm not in the mood. What kind of exams, why? Do you remember what we promised each other? Sincerity! Hell, Novelli, you lectured me, don't you remember?!"

He remained tense, standing above her, with a worried look, the hammock swinging to the right and left, due to the tension imprinted by his strong arms, which he had aimed alongside Francesca's shoulders, who slowly managed to extract the blue stick and white. She turned it for David's to see, but David didn't notice it at first, agitated as he was.

"You're right, you're absolutely right, but I needed confirmation. This morning, I had an ultrasound."

"Oh my God, Franci", the hammock moved a lot, "You... you... what is it? Something ba-"

"No, no," she caressed him, "I'm pregnant, David," she brought the stick to his lively eyes.

"What? No what? Who? What do you?! I-" The hammock began to swing faster.

"Careful, David, don't move too much!"

"Are you telling me that... oh crap... you just

told me that… we are expecting a baby? Another?!"

"Mm… yeah… another Trilli."

David dived into Francesca's arms and kissed her all over, on her neck, chin, ears, nose and she laughed out loud.

"Oh man, Franci! You scared me! Uff… it's beautiful, Franci! I mean, are you okay? Is the little one okay?" Suddenly he looked towards Francesca's belly and tried to stop the hammock which was moving left and right. "Franci, you have to get off. Should we get off? Do you feel like throwing up?"

"Ha, ha, ha, no, no. Don't worry, I'm fine. The nauseas are there, but they will pass. The day after tomorrow I have a visit to the gynecologist. You know, I think I'll have to run those tests, to see if there are-"

David poked a finger at her mouth, panting. "I love you, Franci and we will do everything, we will do everything. You and me together, but we'll think about it tomorrow, Franci. Let's think about everything tomorrow. Now, I want to stay here, breathe in the stars and embrace my dreams."

He squeezed her tightly, put his hand on her stomach and lay down beside her, beginning to hum.

Francesca inhaled deeply and made a happy face. In the air, the taste of David mixed with the scent of September.

Of a sweet September.

*****

Don't miss the other books from Maddi Magrì already available at Amazon!

Giulia's Vineyard
(Italian Romance Stories Vol.1)

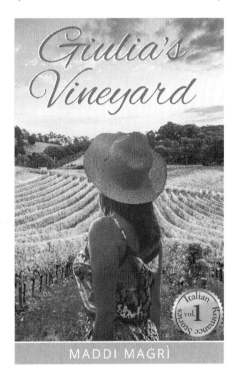

A new beginning. This is what Giulia needs after Paolo and her marriage are taken away from her. And to start over, Giulia leaves Milan and moves to the Marches region in central Italy. There, among rolling hills filled with sunflowers and vineyards, she meets Luca, a charming and witty winemaker. But he, too, has a past to forget.
Will he be the right person for a new chapter in her life?